HEAVEN ON EARTH

By Fadi Zaghmout

Praise for *Heaven on Earth*:

"Fadi Zaghmout's *Heaven on Earth* presents a fascinating vision of a future world devoid of the aging process, merging many themes, including technological, social, and legal that researchers, investors, regulators, and legislators, in today's day and age, must grapple with in lieu of the unavoidable paradigm shift that will be arriving. A must-read for anyone involved directly or tangentially in the age-reversal scientific community"

—Ira S. Pastor, CEO BioQuark Inc., Rejuvenation Biotechnology Company

"In this valuable novel, Fadi Zaghmout puts a personal face to the world we are all longing for (some of us more secretly than others). It is an interesting and realistic read, showing humanity as it has always been but with a new dawn of life where the infirmity of old age is a choice."

—Aubrey de Grey, Chief Science Officer, SENS Research Foundation

"Thought experiment: what if science offered you a golden pill to live longer—much longer than you ever imagined; to turn back time; to bring back your parents, would you take it? Zaghmout takes a look at a future where this is possible and explores its existential implications in the context of family, love, betrayal, and death in an advanced world where humans are still very much as they are today."

—Lara Matossian, founder and CEO of Sci Fest Dubai

"It has been a long time since a book haunted me for months. *Heaven on Earth* did just that. The small details and the local yet universal context of the book got me hooked, and I could hardly put it down while reading. Fadi knows enough about what he is writing about to a point where I could bet that he experienced Janna's arm pain when stretching her arm to get her phone when it fell under one of Amman's local pubs' heavy tables, or her attachment to Sabah's songs.

While sci-fi books sometimes feel more and more pretentious, *Heaven on Earth* breaks that genre's stereotype with a dramatic sour nostalgic edge and in a time where notification sounds could be the sound you hear the most during the day. The book exaggerates those notifications to predict the future of technology, religion, and even sex in the small capital city called Amman."

—Zaid Bawab, Jordanian filmmaker, part-time lecturer, and music curator

"A courageous and creative attempt to address contemporary social problems in the Arab world through science fiction. Brace yourself for an outstanding journey.

—Batir Wardam, Jordanian writer and social-media activist

"Fadi has skillfully interweaved a paradoxical world that is both utopian and dystopian: too advanced, yet extremely relatable and cleverly reflective of the dilemma of our fluid modernity. An intriguing setting, captivating characters, and a provocative plot make you wonder whether we are moving forward to perpetuity or being cast into an eternal purgatory."

—Fadi G. Haddad, Jordanian film director and writer

HEAVEN ON EARTH

By Fadi Zaghmout
Translated from the Arabic by Sawad Hussain

REBEL SATORI PRESS

New Orleans & New York

Published in the United States of America by
Rebel Satori Press
www.rebelsatoripress.com

Originally published in Arabic by Dar Al Adab, Beirut.English
translation first published in 2017 by Signal 8 Press.

Cover design: Cristian Checcanin
Author photo: Salzburg Global Seminar/ Ela Grieshaber

ISBN: 978-1-60864-366-0
eISBN: 978-1-60864-377-6

Author's note:

In 2010, while I was visiting Chicago, a friend of mine asked me to get him that month's copy of *GQ* magazine. I remember I flipping through the copy in my hotel room, reading the headlines, when I noticed an article with a title that said human beings may soon be able to live up to 1000 years and beyond. It was an interview with Aubrey de Grey, the famous English gerontologist who came up with a roadmap for how to defeat aging. The possibility hit me hard, as dying from old age has always been a given, something that is impossible to change. It gave me hope. Thus believing Aubrey's words, I started to imagine: What will life be like when this happens? How will it affect our lives, our morals, and our society? Would be really like heaven when we push death away from us?

A few years later, I finished the story, and it was published in Arabic by Dar Al Adab. And I moved to Dubai, where one day Aubrey de Grey was hosted for a talk at Cafe Scientifique in the city. It was like a dream for me to meet the man who promising us a longer life. There was no way I would have missed that event. I went there and met him and told him how he inspired me to write the book. I emailed him few months later when the English translation was ready and asked him if he would be interested in writing me a book blurb, and he did.

I would like to dedicate this book to him, to thank him for his efforts towards saving humanity from the horrors of old age.

I would also like to dedicate this book to my parents, stating my ultimate dream, my grand wish to see both of them getting back their youth when this technology is materialized.

And a special dedication to everyone in my life, my family members and close friends. I want you all to stay here with me for a long long time. Love you all.

I may not have painted in this book the heaven we dream of, but I hope that the premise of a longer life may give some happiness to all of those who love living and who enjoy their lives here on this planet.

CHAPTER 1

JAMAL'S BIRTHDAY

LIFE'S estrangement from me still lingers; it refuses to embrace me, to take me in its arms and shelter me. The world turns its back on me and feigns ignorance of my needs. It turns a blind eye to my nostalgia for days that seem warmer, more forgiving in my memory, and in the imprints of time where there wasn't a day as cruel as this one. I got used to life's surprises and its lunacy, got accustomed to its blessings and curses, but I still feel its coldness – as if I'm from another place, an entirely different world altogether; as if this life is a land of exile no matter how long I've lived here, how tightly I've held fast to its soil or how deeply I've breathed in its air.

On the one hand, life has been openhandedly generous to me; on the other, it has seized everything and everyone that means anything whatsoever to me. Sometimes it gives without keeping score, and sometimes it freely takes from me. It sweeps me away in its swirling tides of time, a limited period that I've come to see as short, and of whose expiry date I have come to dread. Life though, with its usual sadism, distorted time while recasting it – this time arming it with scientific breakthroughs. Life wanted time to be bitter and long with no tangible end in sight for the mind to latch on to, or apparent signs of the end that the heart could comprehend. The end was always imminently near, possibly just a few hours away even, but today it's become too distant for us to even wrap our heads around.

The ringing chimes of time haven't shown me any mercy, resonating in my ears amidst the tunes of Jamal's birthday and the candles flickering on my brother's cake, his birthday the very same scene every year for as long as I can remember. This year though, the sight of Jamal's weary body across from me insisted on reminding me that time had flown by. His children and grandchildren's radiant faces were gathered around the photo while he sat at the middle of the table behind the cake. His angelic face seemed even paler today as life steadily drained away from his body. And yet he was grinning away as everyone sang, celebrating him.

Their voices rose in unison as they belted out the familiar refrains of "Happy Birthday." At the end of the song I raised the volume of my voice and instead of "to you," sang "to Jamal." I smiled at him when our eyes met. I clapped warmly at the end of the age-old ditty and drew close. I hugged him and kissed his head, whispering, "May you have golden years ahead, sweetie," despite knowing that his days were numbered and that the day of his departure was achingly at hand.

I didn't wish him the usual "I hope you have a hundred birthdays," because he'd already been there, done that. This popular tiding had lost its meaning in an era where being a centenarian was no longer a milestone to which humans aspired. I almost told him "I wish you a thousand more," but caught myself because I knew that he had shouldered the strains of old age with commendable equanimity and was now looking forward to his death.

He had two sons, three grandsons, and a granddaughter from the third generation who was the youngest of us all. Everyone was here at this get-together that I had organized, except for his ex-wife Jihan. She had deserted him fifteen years earlier after her vitality and youthfulness had returned.

I left him to his fawning children and occupied myself with cutting the birthday cake. I got my husband Zaid to help hand out the slices.

A pang stabbed my heart at the idea that Jamal's departure was fast approaching. I felt it more intensely that day than even the pain that had engulfed me when my mother and father died; as I saw it, my parents leaving this world was unavoidable, whereas Jamal dying was preventable.

When Mom passed on from this world after a heart-rending struggle with Alzheimer's in the spring of 2022, we didn't have what it took to overthrow this tyrannical, insidious illness. Likewise, when death snatched my father away under the guise of angina in the summer of 2026, we – mankind – didn't have the solution for weak arteries or the caving of their softening walls over time. Today, however – on Jamal's hundredth birthday on June 8th, 2091 – the magical panacea for aging is now within everyone's reach in the form of a small golden pill that revitalizes the cells in the body, shielding us from aging, along with its hardships and woes.

The synthesis of this pill twenty years ago was undoubtedly a monumental human feat. Its arrival wasn't a complete surprise to us because it was the product of the steady growth of biotechnological knowledge honed through myriad trials of old-age ailment therapies. These efforts resulted in the golden pill that contained state-of-the-art nanobots tasked with reinforcing the human immune system while rejuvenating the productive capacity of the body's cells – in effect, wiping out old age altogether.

My struggle that day with Jamal's illness wasn't with knowledge or scientific capabilities, but instead his principles and values. Nothing stood between me and protecting him, keeping him here by my side in this world, nothing except his moral code and his fantasies of death; fantasies in which he saw the starkness of old age – sickness and rotting away – slip into death, a welcome respite granting freedom and happiness in a hereafter in which he staunchly believed and for which he eagerly yearned.

Tears streamed down my cheeks as I quickly retreated to the kitchen so as not to be a killjoy. I carried a few cake-crumbed plates with me and busied myself with washing them.

When I returned, everyone was quietly seated, eyes glued to a screen displaying a scrolling album of photos from the distant past that Khalid, Jamal's eldest son, had put together for this occasion. The first photo was of Jamal and Jihan in the limo that had transported them on their wedding night over seven decades ago. The couple was holding onto each other. Jamal had a wide grin on his face with his arm comically hooked around Jihan's neck, concealing whether the real sentiment behind his slung arm was intense love or rancor. Jihan came across as strangled, struggling to crack a smile in front of the photographer without letting on whether she was actually giddy about Jamal's horsing around or not.

Jamal cut a debonair figure in his wedding suit, with his clear-cut dimples and perfectly set black hair. Jihan came across as a clown; her features were overdone as usual in heavily layered makeup – even more so that night. What's weird is that after her rejuvenation, she doesn't even share likeness with that picture, taken from Jihan's first round of youth. Jamal heaved a heavy sigh when he set eyes on the photo. He took a deep breath and quoted in a barely audible voice Abu-al-'Atahiya's famous line of poetry: "If only youth were to return one day/ I'd inform him of what old age did."

I almost reminded him about how his youth was primed to return if he wanted, but I stayed silent once his youngest granddaughter saved him from my interjection with one of her own: "And I'm definitely the final shred of evidence of that love!" she joked as she gestured towards the dated photo of the once-happy couple. Everyone burst out laughing as the photo morphed into another, transporting us to the summer of 2052.

There we were, Zaid and I, Jamal and Jihan, Khalid and his wife Meera, encircling Sabah, or Sabuha as her fans fondly called her, on the southern stage of the Jerash music festival. Sabah was wearing, as was expected of a celebrity, a massive dress inlaid with a king's ransom in gems and embroidered with gaudy, gold-colored thread. Her gleaming blonde hair was gigantic, bequeathing her with a halo that reminded me of the sun goddess.

Even though Jihan and I were substantially younger than Sabuha, we looked older than her; she had stridden ahead of us to reclaim her youth at a time when these procedures were still complicated and were advertised at exorbitant prices. As fifty-eight-year-olds, we were younger than her, but here was Jihan with more wrinkles on her face than the famous singer herself! Khalid's wife sneered as she commented on the photo: "According to *Sayadatee*[1] magazine, people say even after all that, Sabuha fell into a depression after her last divorce."

Khalid changed the photo. I don't know why he picked this one, but we ended up appraising a scene from February 2072. It's a horrible photo of Zaid and me hunched over, shrunken, thinning hair just about covering our scalps, our flabby jowls hanging loose. Zaid was leaning on his cane while I was holding a glass of water in my left hand and the golden pill of eternal youth in my right, like a celestial being giving him the first drop from the fountain of youth to drink.

I remember that there was an indescribable joy that day, the day we swallowed the first of those golden pills. Others we knew had gone before us in reclaiming their vim and vigor. We hadn't been far behind, burning with desire to embark on our own journey after old age had sapped us dry.

But to this day, I still can't fully wrap my head around the miraculous effects of this pill that offered us a new lease on youth in just a few months. It was as if I had woken up from a rough dream to a new appreciation for the sensations of life, which had been all but lost to me as I advanced in age.

---

1 My Lady

I clearly remember the first days after strength returned to my body, making it just as limber as it had been during my teenage years. Each day I filled out in all the right places while my energy levels shot up. When I first entered my teenage years, the gradual swelling of my breasts and increase in my height had been sources of pride; this time round, my transformation filled me joy as well as a naked desire to enjoy my own body and that of my husband.

The picture morphed once more and there we were in December 2080. Jamal and I were in the neonatal ward of the hospital for the birth of his last grandchild. The difference between my face in this photo and the previous one was staggering. So was the contrast between Jamal's face in the previous photo with Sabah and this one.

Jamal's face lit up as he cradled his granddaughter in his trembling hands while I stood beside him, propping him up, afraid that she'd slip out of his grasp. His granddaughter joked, "Who's that cutie-pie?" Her mother clutched her tightly to her chest, "Who else but you, honey?"

Khalid saved the best for last. It etched the most profound impression on my soul that night. It was a childhood scene from March 1992. Jamal, then scarcely a year old, was taking his first steps. His legs and thighs were bloated like a sumo wrestler's. His mouth and bib were smeared with copious dollops of chocolate.

My mother crouched behind him in the photo, encircling him with her arms, ready to grab him if he faltered. How my heart ached. How beautiful you were, Mom! What a stunner you were in your youth. How carefree you look in this photo.

You were all life, energy, and love. How unfair that destiny yanked you away from us without giving you a choice to stay. Would you have stayed or left like Jamal wants to? Maybe you being here would have been enough to convince him to stay. Maybe enough to make Dad stay too, and for all of us to be together longer, living an idyllic life filled with your affection and tenderness. How painful memories can be.

Khalid's album was a hefty weight that wore me down, and tired Jamal out as well. He asked his two sons to carry him to his bed so he could get some shut-eye. A few minutes after Jamal had retired to his room, Khalid came back to inform me that Jamal wanted to speak to me about something important. I hurried to his room, anxious about what it could be.

CHAPTER 2

LAW

I SLIPPED into Jamal's room and closed the door behind me. Straightening my back, I tried to inject some bounce into my step as I got nearer to him. I asked, "You out of steam?" He nodded as I pressed on "You're not going to change your mind?" I placed my hand on his forehead and pleaded, "For my sake?" He shook his head, just as he always did whenever I begged him to stay on with us, here.

I wasn't new to trying to convince Jamal in myriad ways. This time I exaggerated for his benefit my happiness at the return of my youth and vitality. I sat next to him, mirror in hand, and compared the clarity of my skin, free from any signs of aging, with his sagging skin and wiry lips. I kissed his forehead now and told him that youth was within arm's reach if he wanted it.

I immediately regretted my actions and scolded myself for my thoughtless peacocking. How could I make him feel so weak? I resented myself when I realized that I had made more arduous for him what was already harsh enough. I regretted my hasty question because I didn't want to ruin tonight of all nights, his birthday. I didn't want to take a stand against him, so I tried to swallow the bitter pill of his decision.

I drew close and gave my moral support, saluting his courage and willpower. I shared my despair and inability to keep going, to keep on living. I whispered in his ear, "You know Jamal, you're strong… not a cop-out like me. I don't have your guts to leave this world behind me." I fell silent, then mused, "Maybe I just don't have your good sense to let nature take its course and take me out."

His face crumpled at my show of fragility. Weeping, he confessed his weakness as well. He poured out his heart to me and said how scared he was to die. "You know, Janna, that I'm a believer in God's fate. But maybe I haven't let on just how scared stiff I am. On the inside, I'm terrified." He said I was the one making it the hardest for him to let go. He tried to reassure me, encouraging me as he slowly stammered faltering, barely audible words. "You're the fighter, Janna, not me. You're the strong one because you're holding onto this world. I'm done for. I've given up."

He tried to comfort me further still by quoting Dad, saying, "There's no good or bad fate; all of us are at the beck and call of the Almighty's wisdom." We both fell silent, realizing the extent of our contradicting desires, and our pusillanimity as we contemplated each other's path to freedom. He broke the silence with a sudden question about Jihan, "Where's Jihan? Why didn't she come? Didn't you invite her?"

His question grated on me so I hastily changed the subject before I blew up in his face. "Did you like the photos that Khalid put together?"

I used to get upset when I couldn't rein myself in, and I would rage at him when silence was his only comeback. I would find it difficult to control my anger when I felt that he still loved her, still yearned for her even after years of being separated, and after her attempts to get her grubby hands on all the family assets. It's as if he forgot how she dropped him and abandoned their marriage, refusing to stand by him through his old age and debility. She left him to me, to take care of in his dark days, after claiming the best years of his life.

I still curse myself for the day I brought her home at the start of my journalism degree course. My mother cursed that day even years after her gradual memory loss had set in. As if that day was one of those seminal moments that she refused to let slip from her consciousness. She was always lamenting, "May God have mercy on Janna for having such a friend."

On that day, Jamal stood behind the door, a fun-loving guy of twenty-two, stunned by Jihan's beauty as if he were seeing one of heaven's promised rewards for the righteous, the gorgeous siren-like *houris* that destiny had sculpted to cloud his mind. I remember all too well his stutter when I introduced her to him as my friend from college. I can't forget how nervous he was, apologizing for his cotton undershirt and itty-bitty shorts that he had gotten used to lounging in around the house.

Completely out of character, he sat with us at lunch and was somewhat hospitable. Mom and I weren't aware that he was even capable of such a thing. And when the time came for her to leave, he didn't miss a beat as he offered his services as a chauffeur to drop her home in the Al-Jubayhah neighborhood in his then-new Mercedes, which truthfully piqued her interest more than his entire existence.

Simply put, he was head over heels from their first meeting. At that moment, I had to admit to myself that his all-encompassing attraction to her had turned him to jelly.

Hell-lady, as I like to call Jihan, had bewitched him from their first encounter without even acknowledging his presence. I'm almost certain that she still didn't truly *see* him even after more than fifty years of marriage. He was, in her opinion, just like everything else in her life, a tool to exploit for her own selfish whims. She was only concerned about him when it was somehow linked to her well-being, and would belittle him if he opposed her designs. So Jamal the doctor, the genetic-diseases specialist, a wealthy man from a good family, well regarded among mere acquaintances and friends, became the Jamal who neither knew how to wear his shirt nor choose his food whenever he failed to win Jihan's approval.

Despite her bite easing up as age took its toll on her, she wasted no time in ingesting the golden pill without sparing a thought for Jamal or her kids. In a matter of months, her youthfulness returned and, with it, her robustness and her haughtiness – maybe even more so.

We would usually laugh at Jamal and keep on reminding him of how he didn't have a problem using Viagra – the blue pill – when he needed it, so why was he now discriminating between pills and steering clear of the golden one?

As for Hell-lady, she couldn't say no to any type of pill that would increase her strength. But I can swear not only with my pinky, but my thumb, my index finger – heck, all my fingers on both hands – that she's totally lost it with the rena-scence of her youth! It seemed her inordinate obsession with grabbing people's attention during her girlhood had grown stronger, tenfold. No amount of time was able to heal the complexity of her childhood, however much she fashioned her appearance or altered her features. Her need to be the cynosure of all eyes, in my humble opinion, was an extension of her losing her father at a tender age, which transformed her over time into a despicable being, clueless as to how to garner respect except by imposing her will and bragging about what she owned.

Today, in the second round of her youth, she's started to overplay it by wearing outfits that over-accentuate her wom-anly curves and slapping on makeup that magnifies the few visible wrinkles that she does have. It's her way of saying to those around her, "Look at me!" I figure it's this clown-like get-up that singles her out today, especially after we've lost the ability to make out her real features. Going by the fashionable shape of her nose, her overly sculpted lips, or her in-vogue cheeks lauded on the pages of the fashion magazines, the dif-ference is like that between night and day.

But I wonder: Is it in mankind's best interest to supply this eternal youth elixir to everyone without any selection cri-teria or exceptions? Does it equally bestow youth on those who have a sensible head on their shoulders and those who don't? Isn't it unfair that we lose people with Jamal's virtue while others with Hell-lady's vices stay on in this world?

What's the long-term outcome of this in a society that obstinately believes in reward and punishment in the hereafter? The virtuous individuals long for their rewards in the hereafter whereas the evil ones run away from their punishment by clinging to the physical world and staying here among us.

Why is it difficult for us to convince those with good hearts to stay? Why does human invention insist on privileging those who are less humane? How will this planet look after a few decades if everyone who is good and decent insists on leaving?

Enough with my pessimistic ranting. I mean, mankind has always been able to keep its unjust side in check throughout history, however powerful this side has gotten and no matter how many vestiges it has left on the pages of history. It will probably take some time, but if we're capable of convincing kind-hearted people to stay here on Earth, then maybe they can guide those of us who are still here, who have lost our moral compass. If a century wasn't enough to set Hell-lady's faults right, then maybe the centuries to come hold the solution for such characters.

Hold on, did I say centuries? Jihan and me? On the same planet? God no! If only I could persuade Jamal. If I could just convince him to stay...

But I knew it was impossible to change his mind when I found out why he had asked me to come to his bedroom that evening. He didn't want to ask about Jihan. Instead he wanted to talk to me about the new bill pending before parliament.

Parliament was debating whether to enact a law that would force those over sixty years of age to take the golden pill and roll back the years. The proposed law reflected the change that had occurred in public opinion towards the concept of aging as a curable ailment, not as a natural state that was beyond repair. The law was based on pure economics, aiming to save Jordan a fortune in dinars spent on taking care of people too old to participate in the development of the national economy.

Lately there had been a competition among government-financed authors to support the bill. Each one extrapolated their arguments from an idea that had started to gain traction in social and religious circles: the concept that refusing the available treatment was akin to suicide – a societal disgrace. On the other hand, several independent writers and thinkers argued for the principle of individual freedom and the individual's right to choose life or death regardless of society's need for that person.

Jamal had already chosen death and had borne pain for several years. His greatest dream was about to be snatched away from him by this bill. Society wanted to chain him down in a world that he wanted to escape.

He surprised me when his eyes brimmed with tears as he read from the latest bulletin. His body quaked and his speech faltered. He agonizingly pleaded with me, "Janna, people listen to you. I beg you, stop this bill from passing." He looked at me with an intensity that didn't match the physical or psychological states that I had gotten used to seeing him in lately. "I want to die. It's all too much for me."

At these words, I was convinced that his fate was sealed and that he was sincerely ready to die. I clasped his hand, reassuring him that I was behind him, but my heart was gripped with fear at the thought of him leaving me. No one could assure me that I'd be able to survive without my brother.

I stood shackled by his persistence and stubbornness, weak against life's injustice as I always was and, it seems, always will be as long as I'm game for living in this world.

CHAPTER 3

BACK TO CHILDHOOD

SOMETIMES it seems to me that man is just like a child who pulls apart and ruins anything before him that he doesn't fully understand; he might pluck out a doll's hair because like a baby, he doesn't know what the doll is for; or he may chew on its head because he sees it as a morsel of candy. Or tear apart the doll's clothes, transforming it into a stark rod that will be inevitably discarded once the "fun factor" wears off. What if man suddenly found himself face to face with one of the greatest discoveries in human history – a discovery he would degrade into a mere plaything after having left it at the mercy of his inchoate understanding? How can we comprehend the inventions of those who, to human minds, are experts in a money-hungry society, where our inquisitive human nature has elevated reality TV into one of the cornerstones of popular entertainment?

The outcome was inevitable for this new reality television show, *Born Again with a Golden Spoon*. The show's premise was pretty simple, really, considering how we're now capable of reprogramming our ageing body cells to spawn adolescent - and even embryonic - progeny. Someone thought that since we humans adored competition and controlling each other's lives, and as there were a number of poverty-stricken individuals in the country ready to do whatever it took to attain a better life, wouldn't it be great if they brought together twenty competitors in a reality TV show to duke it out during their return "trip" to childhood, to the first day of life itself?

Going by the viewers' votes, after having taken the pill, the most popular child would win a grand prize of 50 million dinars, guaranteed to keep the winner rolling in money for at least the next two centuries. Zaid and I were eager to watch the first episode tonight after the frothy storm the media whipped up about it. Dog-tired after a long day at work and not in the mood for a heavy dinner, we decided to instead munch on some *labney* sandwiches with a cup of tea. Jamal couldn't stay up much later, so he retired early to bed claiming that he could wait and watch the show the next morning.

The show started after about half an hour of advertisements; the appreciation of time, just like there isn't any respect for the viewer, had become but ancient history. After the introductory song, the Lebanese host welcomed us with a vivid presentation of the great dream that the "intrepid" – as she dubbed them – yearned for, after which the competitors came in. Each one gave us a glimpse into their world through a brief introductory video clip showing their harsh living conditions: Salma, Dayana, Omar, Qwaidar, Bashar, and so on. Competitors of all ages, all of them poor, and – in line with the show's rules – not having had the golden pill before.

Interspersed between the clips of each competitor was a cartoon of a smiling kid grasping a golden spoon that he waved rather enthusiastically. The reel was bookended by one final flourish of the kid cackling as he winked theatrically at the audience. I really didn't know what to make of the theatrics.

Salma, who shared that she was from the town of Russeifa, was the first to flash across the screen with her crooked back, white hair, and threadbare clothes. Directing her speech to the audience, she said, "Baba was paralyzed in a car accident the day I was born. Mama never worked a day in her life. We were starving and young, waiting for one of the neighbors to take pity on us and feed us. When Baba died, Mama disappeared. She just took off, leaving behind my sister and me to our fate. We were still so young, and we didn't know how to survive except by going out on the streets, stretching out our hands to people, begging them to help us." Salma looked out the studio to an audience moved by her words. "I hope you all will help me today, and give me another chance at a life that I can maybe live out better... live a life just like I've seen those who give me money have."

Despite my towering curiosity, I was disgusted by the whole idea of the show even before it started. How could the producers allow themselves to exploit these contestants' dire straits in this undignified way? Instead of the promised new beginning for the impoverished, I could only see a mature person being killed, a murder of his current and fully formed identity on the pyre of conversion into an entirely different person. Returning back to one's childhood, as we know it these days, erases the memory. These contestants wouldn't know a thing about their pasts except what has been preserved of their memories in the electronic files.

"Maybe it's better for them? What would they want with painful memories?" Zaid offered as he strangely defended the show's premise.

"But doing it like this means we've stolen their identities. We've erased them from the world," I countered, unconvinced if my answer was enough to be accepted as logical. Which identity was I talking about? Their identity as poor people formed from their life experience and personality, as Zaid had said? Or an identity borne of "age," one that they were as free to choose as we all had been before them? Or could it be their preserved genetic code that supposedly would be reshaped in a better environment and with a brighter future this time round?

Omar, the second contestant, drew my attention back to the show. Omar, whom I had known since my days in college: as a kid of ten or eleven, he would sneak onto campus with his older brother, clutching chewing-gum packets to sell to the students.

I remember what first drew me to him was his self-respect at that age: he would refuse to take any money unless it was the price of a stick of gum that he was selling, albeit at a price ten times higher than its real worth.

Omar had changed over time. He had become somewhat pushy when his childhood innocence no longer helped him in tugging at the heartstrings of those around him. With his natural shrewdness, he replaced his boyish innocence with a strategic smile and sugary words.

By the time he had grown into a man, the traffic light at the entrance of the Abdoun residential area had become his firm companion. It was as if his destiny and livelihood were tied to this traffic light, as they had been with the chewing-gum packets that had been with him since childhood. Oh, here's the traffic light in his intro clip, I thought to myself as the video rolled. And there's the manufacturer of that gum he used to sell, appearing as one of the show's official sponsors.

The whole world around him was changing while he remained just the same, growing older each day, in his hand the same packets of gum.

When I started university, Omar was selling gum. I graduated and Omar was selling gum. I travelled to the United States to do my master's and came back after two years to find Omar at the same traffic light, selling the same old gum. I worked as a journalist making my way up that job ladder, and there was Omar selling gum at the traffic light as always. I got to know Zaid; we got engaged, and then married. I founded my own newspaper that flourished, spread, then ended up on its last legs... and Omar hadn't changed. I lost Mom, Dad, but I never lost a day of Omar's presence and his morning smile at the traffic light. I grew old and retired, no longer strong enough to go out on a daily basis, but Omar, even in his old age and feebleness, never let down his traffic light or the chewing gum that would sweeten his customers' mouths, allowing him to connect with the world around him. When I regained my strength, Omar was there waiting for me also, just as he always was, at the traffic light, and in his hand –

what do you know, packets of gum!

After all this, didn't people like him deserve a second chance at life? How many times had I wished to myself that I had a magic wand to banish his poverty and transform his life? I grew immune to those guilty feelings that would trail me every day at the traffic light, me in my swanky car, chewing away on the gum from his very hands.

"May God grant you success and keep you happy, Miss Janna," he would always pray for me. I would respond, as usual, "May He also grant you success, and keep you safe as He wills, Omar." I would then take some change worth more than the gum out of my wallet, consider it charity, and self-consciously slip it into his hand.

His prayer for me changed over the years as age caught up with me, its hints indelibly etched on my body, "May God grant you exceeding health all your life, Janna." I'd respond "May He extend your life and keep you with us, sir."

Hell-lady would chide me in those days: "Don't look at him, people like him are richer than you and me both, darrrling," or, "By doing this, you're encouraging him to beg." I never seemed to have a comeback. If he *really* was richer than both of us, as she claimed, why insist on a life of begging? Why insist on the cruel life he was living? But she wouldn't change her mind, as it was easier for her to convince herself that he was rich, posing as a needy beggar to stir up feelings of guilt within her. In her book, the world was full of greed, more greed, and deception. This was her internal justification for lusting after money and power.

Maybe this was his chance to finally be richer than

Hell-lady and me. I mean, he had been a cute kid growing up, from what I remember, and his great personality would pull in the viewers and their votes. Yes, I thought to myself, if there's someone who deserves a second chance at life, it's definitely Omar.

CHAPTER 4

SEVENTY YEARS

"YOU think Omar has a chance at winning?" I asked Zaid while following the show but he didn't answer. I looked at him and repeated, "Zaid, you think Omar has a chance?"

"Zaid..." I raised my voice, "Zaid!" I hated the feeling of him ignoring me when I spoke to him. As I mused over if he was purposely ignoring me or if he was lost in thought, he quietly answered, "God, I don't know... maybe."

I stretched out my hand and picked a piece of chocolate from the plate on the table just in front of me. I unwrapped it and popped it in my mouth, trying to stifle my irritation. I fell silent momentarily, but I couldn't control myself. I waved my hand in front of the screen to lower the show's volume, and asked him, "Where are you right now? What's the matter?"

My question startled him as if he had never been distracted in the first place. He quickly retorted, "No, no, I'm here, not lost in thought. Everything's fine." He got up and padded into the kitchen. This ticked me off even more; I wanted to follow him to the kitchen to lay into him, but I kept my cool.

I took a deep breath and tried to resume watching the show. My anger didn't let me focus. My eyes were trailing the contestants' movements, whereas my mind was boiling, irritated. This wasn't the first time that Zaid had behaved like this, and he knew damn well that I couldn't stand feeling that there was something he was hiding from me.

I couldn't keep quiet when he resurfaced from the kitchen with a glass of water. "Zaid, what's the matter?" I inquired resolutely this time. He halted in front of me and shook his head in denial. "I swear nothing's wrong, just a tad tired is all."

I gave him a long stare and turned my face away, so that there would be no chance for the tears I felt forming to show. I tried to drain my words of feeling as I continued. "You haven't been yourself for a while now. You know how I hate feeling that you're hiding something from me." Zaid was silent for a little while. Then he looked at me and reasserted that he wasn't hiding anything. He withdrew from the lounge, took a shower, and, after half an hour, retired to the bedroom earlier than usual. He left me to stay up late with my thoughts. I felt utterly confused about us.

Something within me wanted to rise up and scream, even if that meant turning what had just happened into a huge issue between us, but another part of me urged me to stay quiet and deal with the situation rationally. It's simple really, Janna, and doesn't deserve such a hostile reaction, it urged. It was possible he was being honest and there really was nothing to hide.

But his coldness stung me, maybe because it hadn't come out of nowhere, maybe because several issues alluding to a rupture had cropped up recently. Maybe I'm not being exact when I say recently because I'd felt a change in the nature of my relationship with Zaid over the past two years, or even more. I tried to reassure myself that it was a temporary change like any episode of feelings that we had gone through in our long marital life together. I mean, we didn't get married yesterday, and during our relationship there had always been rough patches that resembled what we were going through that day. We normally worked through them and moved on.

But the desire within me then to put an end to our relationship was stronger than any other I had felt in the past. Voices of doubt about our compatibility shook my core with an intensity that I wasn't used to.

Our compatibility? Did I really doubt it after all these years? Did I want to live the next one hundred years with Zaid? And, if I wanted that, what about the hundred years after that? It was easy to suppress those niggling voices when old age was a part of the equation, because old age made one feel lacking, needy. Our relationship had transformed into one of companionship rather than of love. That beautiful companionship was enough at a time when our lives were limited and the end was creeping into sight. But that day, I longed for a bit of romance, for a bit of passion, for a bit of that thirst that you find in the honeymoon phase of relationships.

I went round in a circle and asked myself again, could I live without Zaid? Was it possible to allow myself to risk losing him? The thought of him disappearing from my life scared me just as much as the idea that there *was* a chance to feel happier with someone else. It was an alarming conflict I found myself in, at which I stared helplessly. A conflict eerily similar to my fear of choosing an eternal death instead of the eternal life I lead.

My heartbeat sped up and I fell short of breath; I found myself at a loss, unable to make such a life-altering decision. My chest muscles constricted. My forehead broke out in a sweat and I was tormented when I envisioned life and my misery at its perpetual nature. Life whispered in my ear the bitter truth: that I didn't have, and would never have, the means to change anything at all. Unhappiness, it seemed, was to be my eternal lot.

I headed to the bedroom and stopped at the door, looking intently at Zaid. He was fast asleep, curled up in an embryonic pose under the duvet. His two hands were clasped together across his chest, as if he was praying. His legs were glued together, folded close to this chest. This was the same scene that had repeated itself every night for the past seventy years.

Seventy years we'd been together. Every day, we'd wake up together, eat breakfast, go to our separate worlds at the same time, come back at night to eat dinner together and sleep in the same bed. Zaid was no longer my life partner, but instead he had become *my life:* my identity and my being. The idea of splitting up with him scared the hell out of me.

I got into bed next to him, curled my body in the same direction he was in, and inched closer. Somewhat hesitantly, I put my hand on his shoulder and let it hang, eventually encircling his waist. Out of character, I hugged him and felt somewhat sheepish about it. I put my head at the nape of his neck and let myself cry.

Does he feel what I feel? I wondered. Do these same distressing thoughts come to him that go round and round in my head? Or deep down has he already taken a stand, and started to gradually withdraw from my life? Is this why exhaustion and depression seem to have been weighing him down for the past few days?

I had to talk to him, to understand what was going on in his head, and that's why I decided to confront him. I wouldn't let him get out of facing me the next day. He'll have to tell me everything going on in his head even if it spells the end of us, I resolved as I drifted off to sleep.

Chapter 5

Mom's Resurrection

I WAS alone, as far as I knew, in a house resembling our own on the old family farm that we owned in the Al-Alouk area. The room was semi-dark; the world outside wreathed in darkness, accompanied by the whoosh of the strong winds shaking the trees, windows, and doors. From a distance I heard a sorrowful cat meowing, as if it were mourning, tormented by something or the other, or seized with intense dread.

After a few moments, the sound of a familiar weeping severely unnerved me and made me tremble with grief – it was Mom crying. I hurried to the room next door, which was also dark. I became aware of Mom sitting on the edge of the bed, sobbing violently. For the briefest of moments, I felt comforted seeing her being able to sit on her own, but her wailing unhinged me, just as her tears did.

I approached her and my heart pleaded, "Don't cry... Mom... Mom... don't cry." Her body was emaciated, the bones in her chest jutting out from under her nightdress, her face twisted, her protruding eyes harboring a deep sadness. I extended my arm towards her head to draw it to my chest; maybe I could alleviate her pain. But as soon as I had gotten close enough to touch her, she disappeared into thin air.

After that, the scene changed. I felt her inside me, kicking me forcefully, the brightness of the lightning flashes outside accompanied by the rumbling of thunder. I felt a great weight. I was tired and afraid, as if there was someone who wanted to steal her away from me, snatch her from my womb, and keep us apart.

I heard the sound of a door opening and closing, and in my mind I was convinced that Zaid was with me at the farm, but actually he had deserted me. I almost caught up with him to tell him that I felt labor pains, but for Mom's image appearing in the window behind me. She was an angel, the light of my world. Seeing her brought back in a rush the old comforting feelings I embraced whenever she whispered in a voice I remembered so well, "I'm here, Janna... here I am, alive, well."

I looked at her in disbelief. "Mom, my dearest," I cried, smiling. I stood still and asked her, "You're really okay?"

She beamed and responded, "I'm really okay, and how I've missed you. Come here, let me hug you." The bed separated me from her likeness in the window, but despite the fetus's weight in my abdomen, I hurried to skirt around the bed without noticing the wooden trunk on the ground. I felt my feet collide into the trunk as I ran towards her, my body staggering after losing its balance. My head fell forward, violently crashing into my mom's chest, which disintegrated with the glass shattering, whose sharp shards piercing me all over. I fell forward on my stomach after crashing my head into the window. I was in agony. I yelled without knowing if it was out of fear or pain; a deep resounding yell coupled with the feeling of my soul leaving my body.

I didn't know then if my collision with the apparition of Mom meant we had reunited in the afterlife or if I had been separated from her, now that she was in my womb. I realized it was a separation from both her and the fetus in my womb when Zaid shook me through the duvet, bringing me back to reality.

He said I had been rambling on in the dream and that I had seemed spooked. I looked at him taken aback, trying to comprehend the current shift between the two worlds, as well as the potent emotions that I had wrenched from that world into this one. I turned over in the duvet and away from him, replaying the events of the dream that I could recall. Mom's image in the window and her voice, "Here I am, alive." Those two had the greatest impact on me, as well as her sobbing in pain that reminded me of how distressed I was during the days of her illness.

Often I dreamed of her alive, beautiful, and in robust health. Most of the time, she appeared silent, sitting in the living room of our age-old house, or holding a brush and repainting one of her canvases hanging on our walls, or she was hugging Dad, kissing his cheek each time he returned from Riyadh to visit us during one of the holidays. I still refused to accept her death after all these years. She, too, missed me, and came to visit me from time to time.

I shifted my arm and rested my hand on my stomach

under the duvet, the feeling of having her inside of me still with me, an indescribable feeling. A strange comfort I didn't know from before settled over me, or maybe I had known it from some day in the far past when her presence had been real. I let my soul cling to this comfort and I was lost in that dream that had been chasing me for some time, since I realized that science had become capable of bringing her back to me.

But I remembered Jamal and my thoughts strayed to a place I tried to escape from. I had a commitment to fulfill, to face Jamal before it was too late, before time robbed me and denied me the dream that was consuming me. How embarrassed I feel every time I think of this possibility. It scares me to think of bringing this idea to life, an idea which I can only describe as insanity!

Many times, I allowed my imagination to take complete control of the wheel and plan out the future of my great dream – Mom's comeback! Jamal and I owned the exclusive rights to her genetic map, and a doctor had already confirmed that nothing prevented me from being the incubator of the egg that needed stimulating, the egg that would recreate Mom. Scientifically, it was easy enough, really, a routine operation not considered unusual. But my dilemma was a legal and societal one.

Legally, new births were now forbidden in a bid to control the population growth rate. Pregnancy and giving birth weren't allowed except in one case only: after the loss of a family member. Every family therefore had the right to keep itself from dying out, as well as the right to bring in a newborn to replace a dead family member. Nothing more.

We were on the verge of losing a family member, as Jamal had chosen death. I swore that I would do the impossible to keep him alive if he wanted, but he's stubborn and doesn't want to stay alive. When he passes on, the family will have one opportunity for a newborn. As the rightful heirs of this opportunity, the right won't be exclusive to only me, but also up for grabs by his children and grandchildren. Here was the societal challenge.

It might be inappropriate to broach this topic with Jamal in his final days, as if I might seem to be telling him to hurry up and die so that I could realize this procreative dream of mine. But I had to resolve the issue while he was still here, especially as his passing would mean I would have to confront and convince all his family members, including Jihan, which could turn into an ugly feud I could do without.

Just as I didn't know what his reaction would be, I didn't know how Zaid or the rest of the family would react when I revealed to them that I did not want to give birth – as custom demanded – to a baby whose genetic code was a cocktail of Zaid's and mine. Instead I was planning the resurrection of my mother by using her entire genetic map as the basis for regeneration.

I felt enormously guilty when I thought of Zaid. After all, I had been the reason for us not having any children. How could I be so selfish and tell him that this child wouldn't carry his genes?

CHAPTER 6

REFUSAL TO PROCREATE

I t was a condition I stipulated a few months after we had met. I decided to let him know when we were alone in the tony Irish Bar where we had gotten used to hanging out back then, at the entrance of the Sweifieh area.

I remember my hesitation about broaching this serious matter with him, an emotion similar to the fear that now gripped me when I thought about telling him my decision to give birth to my mother. At that time, I knew well enough that there was a good possibility that I would lose him if I stuck to my guns; now, I knew this possibility still hung in the air. In both cases, I was psychologically ready to accept this loss. At that time I felt reserved, because my decision seemed strange in the eyes of those around me; today I feel even more so, embarrassed even, because I'm preparing to reveal another side of my insanity.

I waited for his last gulp of beer to go down and I hurried to finish mine. I was glued to Zaid under the dim bar lights in the right-hand corner of the bar. The faint music in the background set a calm romantic mood that helped calm my nerves. His hand was next to mine, outstretched on the table, clutching a beer. I calmly moved my fingers and brushed them softly across his fine forearm hair. Then I mustered up the courage to whisper, "Zaid."

I didn't pull off calling his name in the casual manner that I wanted to and his turn towards me, allied with my high-strung nerves, caused my phone to fall off the table. I found myself straining to pick it up from the small gulf between our table and me, a stout table that turned out to be quite heavy and difficult to move. I bent my back and tried to stretch out my hand to get to it, but I felt a shooting pain in my shoulder. "Arghhh," I shrieked as I jerked my hand backwards. Zaid chortled and stretched out his hand this time, patting my shoulder. He then got up calmly, rounded the table from the other side, crouched under it and grabbed my phone. He raised it up to me, his grin never leaving his face. "Here you go."

I took the telephone from his hand and set it on the table. I grudgingly thanked him. My nerves didn't let me see the lighter side of what had just happened. He came back and sat down beside me. "Okay, what's up? Why the extra-long face?"

I took a deep breath and looked at him, "I've made a decision and I have to tell you what it is. I don't know what you'll think."

"What's the decision?"

I fell silent for a moment. I wasn't strong enough to look him in the eye. I started tracing circles with my index finger on the screen of my phone until I worked up the guts to say coldly, "Zaid, I don't want to have kids."

His knee-jerk reaction was to respond as if he were trying to absorb what I had said to him by parroting it back: "What, you don't want to get pregnant and have kids?"

I nodded, fighting back the tears welling up in my eyes. He looked surprised but steadily asked, "And why not?"

"I'm just telling you in case we get, you know, official in the future."

"Okay, but *why* is what I want to know."

"Zaid, how'd we get to know each other?"

"From that Facebook group."

"The group for supporting families of Alzheimer's sufferers."

"Right."

"Your father and my mother both have Alzheimer's, and you know that it's genetic. Mom got it when she was relatively young, meaning the disease runs in the family. Imagine if one of our kids got it?"

"I don't want to think about it. It could also not happen. Why all this doom and gloom? It could happen to you, it could also happen to me, but does that mean we break up and not love anyone else because it *may* happen?"

"No, I didn't say that. I've totally fallen for you, and I'll deal with it if it happens, but honey, I won't carry the guilt of bringing a child into this world just to torture it."

"Okay, but the kid could also get run over or get burnt, or get cancer, God forbid, or anything else. A person doesn't stop living because something *may* happen in the future."

"Because of all that you've listed and more. I'm sorry. I just can't."

"Enough, Janna. I want kids."

That day, the conversation ended with lines drawn sharply between us. Zaid couldn't understand my insistence on not having kids. He couldn't understand me and how scared I was of walking this path and its consequences at that point in time, but my fear of Alzheimer's was worse. So, on top of knowing for certain the truth that I was on the verge of ending this relationship that meant the world to me, was the reality that I might not find another man ready to sacrifice his desire to have kids and confront society's predominant convention? Or would I have to keep this choice of mine under wraps?

After a period of separation that dragged on for two months, and after tasting what it was like to miss me, Zaid gave in. He came back and patched things up between us. In a matter of months, we were rushing our wedding preparations before time beat us to it and stole what was left of my mother- and his father's cognizance.

After some years and with the advent of an Alzheimer's cure, Zaid tried again to convince me to have a kid that would bear our name and help us in our old age. But the idea was even more unsettling for me now that I had passed forty. I refused vehemently and left him to lament over his dream of having children, which I had denied him.

CHAPTER 7

HOURS, HOURS

DEPRESSING is what dawn is when you open your eyes, only to remember that your shoulders are weighed down by burdens you're afraid to get rid of, cumbersome as they are. You may find companionship in the gloomy weather when its darkness and stormy disposition collide, or when the storm intensifies with the growing roar of thunder and lightning flashes. But you can also feel lonely or even cheated when the weather betrays you and greets you with a beaming morning instead. It's like the world has turned its back on you, and as if the storms that ravage your world are only illusions that, to anyone else, mean nothing.

When I opened my eyes that morning, sun rays were streaming through my bedroom window, covering my forehead and face. Usually I liked the tickle of the soft morning rays, gentle and tender like a mother announcing the dawning of a new day. But I was tuckered out, not having slept much during the night. Missing Mom kept me up, and the idea of me being pregnant with her kept gnawing at me. It was a burden whose weight I had gotten used to as the years went by, but today its heaviness increased with the approaching time to claim inheritance of the birth-giving opportunity, and my decision to face Zaid on the matter.

Groggily I got up, took a quick shower and then sat down in front of my dressing mirror and searched for my comb, but as usual I didn't find it where it should have been. I grabbed my smartwatch and pulled it to my mouth, asking, "Where's my comb?"

With a forced smile, Zaid comment dryly before leaving the bedroom, "Whenever I see you, that watch is right next to your mouth. You remind me of my grandma, God rest her soul. She used to yell over the phone when talking to someone overseas. You don't need to bring it right next to your mouth, it'll pick up on your command from a distance."

I almost quipped back, but matched his false smile instead before turning round and round in circles until the red focal point on the electronic lens in my eye landed on Zaid's pants draped on the chair in front of me.

"How on earth did it get under your pants?" Grumbling, I picked up the comb and passed it through my wet hair before I plopped back down in front of the mirror.

Zaid reappeared at the bedroom door. "Do you want me to send the car back for you after I reach the office? I was thinking of sending it for cleaning," he offered.

"No, no I'm off to the office today. I'll catch the metro," I said. I calmly added, as I contemplated my reflection, "Zaid, I have to talk to you about something important. Let's meet after work in the evening and go out for dinner."

He fell silent for a moment, then hesitantly replied, "Sure, me too. I also have something I want to talk to you about." My heart thumped at how he had said it, making me remember last night's delusions.

I picked up my comb and then tapped my finger on my watch screen, tracing a circle on the news ticker from the watch so that it would appear on the e-lens in my eye, allowing me to skim the headlines as I combed. The entire front page of *Al Rai* newspaper – 'The Opinion'- popped up with the following headlines:

US PRESIDENT KHADIJA SALMAN MEETS WITH JORDANIAN KING HUSSEIN II TO DELIBERATE PUSHING PEACE PROCESS FORWARD IN THE REGION

I ignored this news item. What was the point of these talks after the Arab-Israeli conflict was going on two centuries with no end in sight? It seemed like this perpetual conflict also took a golden pill and kept on renewing itself with the turnover of political leaders in the region and the world at large.

CONSULTATIVE COMMITTEE MEETING
FOR PARLIAMENT AND HOUSE OF
REPRESENTATIVES TO DISCUSS CONSENSUAL
ELECTORAL LAW

Like the Arab-Israeli conflict, reaching a consensual electoral law acceptable to all political powers in this country seemed a pipe dream.

JORDANIAN GIRL MURDERED BY BROTHER UNDER GUISE OF HONOR

Although this particular piece of news had been cropping up every few months ever since I could make out the alphabet, it upset me all the same. I thought time itself was enough to guarantee the burying of this ugly killing culture, but it proved to me sadly that putting an end to honor crimes would be infinitely harder than getting rid of old age.

RETURN TO CHILDHOOD SHOW RACKS UP HIGHEST VIEWERSHIP DURING ITS FIRST EPISODE

I focused on the photo gallery accompanying this more pleasant article and blinked to open it. The collection of photos fanned out before me. Omar appeared in more than one of them in the background and clearly in two. One of them was of him at that traffic light in Abdoun, bent over, clothes threadbare, next to a SUV, handing a piece of gum to the driver; in the second, he was onstage next to the show's host. His leathery face, though creased with wrinkles, came across as glowing on stage, with a smile I was used to seeing dancing on his lips.

I set the hairdryer to one side and hurriedly voted for him. Shortly after, I busied myself with plastering his photo all over my social media accounts. I blinked on the typing button and a projected holographic keyboard lit up on my desk. I added a few words next to the picture: *Please everyone, vote for my friend Omar. I've known this guy since college and I know firsthand his lifelong struggle with poverty. I've known this guy since college and I know firsthand his life-long struggle with poverty. Maybe I'm being biased, but I've never seen him frown on any given morning. There hasn't been a single day where I've spoken to him and he didn't respond beaming, with a prayer for me. Not one day did I read class resentment or despair on his face.*

I bowed to him out of respect for his zest for life, even though I still stood unable to grasp his ability to hang onto hope for a better future after having tasted many bitter days for more than eighty years. It might have been masochism that pushed him to cling onto this world, but it was a natural type of masochism, one that everyone knows well, at least those of us who made the choice to remain here and forever young – hanging on no matter how unhappy we felt.

I saw a semblance of injustice in the show's insistence on each participant going back to the first day of their lives, but I was also sure that it was the participant's individual choice and personal right to do so. Despite my ambivalent moral standpoint toward the show, I found myself with a personal duty to support Omar. Maybe it was to compensate for all those years where I couldn't really help him, and maybe one of his childhood dreams would come true: he was getting another shot at life, this time with a golden spoon to make up for what had already happened.

I hit the send button and then moved onto another headline that grabbed my attention:

JORDANIAN PARLIAMENT PREPARES TO
DISCUSS SUICIDE PROHIBITION LAW

Following the news was an article penned by Jihan, her title adapted from a Quranic verse: *Don't kill yourselves for God has been merciful to you.*[2] Beside the article was a "Most Read" tag, with an average rating of very good, and a recent photo of Jihan. At first, I thought there was some kind of mistake because her features in the photo strayed from what I knew. Her hair had transformed, a lurid golden color in the shape of a lion's mane. I knew that hairstyle well because it was all over Amman lately, but Jihan as usual went over the top. The sheer size of the hair around her head was twice that of any other woman with the same coiffure. I added the article to my future reading list and deleted it from the house network, ensuring Jamal wouldn't read it.

I put my watch in my palm again, brought it to my mouth and said "Hours, hours... Sabah." Her voice burst forth into the room: "Hours Hours/ Hours Hours/ I love my days and I adore my life." I opened my wardrobe and chose a loose black skirt along with a white chiffon blouse. I put them on and stopped by Jamal's room to bid him good morning. I brought him breakfast and kissed his forehead. I made sure he put on his wristband – the one linked to the Internet that measured his vital signs – before I left the house. I almost brought up the issue of inheriting his right to life and how I wanted to get

---

2 Surah An-Nisa (4:29)

pregnant, but I faltered. It would be better if I spoke to Zaid about the matter first.

As I left his room, I heard Sabah crooning: "And hours hours/ How alone I feel/ How the words on my tongue aren't new/ How unhappy I am/ I'm not happy…" I sang along with her, "I'm not happy, not happy," and felt my tears stream down. She finished: "Heavy is time's footstep/ Heavy is time's ticking."

I sighed and whispered to myself, "Oh Sabuha, yes, how heavy are the hands of time."

CHAPTER 8

THE SAME SCENE

I GLANCED at my watch to check that I wasn't late for my appointment at the office. I had to pick up my pace to catch the metro; the station was five minutes away from our home in Abdoun. Our three-floor house was home to three families. On the first floor were Zaid, Jamal, and myself. Jamal joined us after Jihan had deserted him and he was no longer strong enough to live on his own; this was same floor where we had lived out our childhood. The second floor had been home to Jamal's family for a number of years, and was now the home of his namesake – his grandson Jamal – and his family. On the third floor lived Khalid – Jamal's firstborn son – and his family; they had been there for a while.

The newspaper office's location in the al-Abdali area was really convenient for me, just another five minutes on the metro. I usually made the most of this time by people-watching and reading the electronic biodata of whoever piqued my interest.

Today something weird happened that I could not explain.

I felt my heart pounding the moment I saw the young man sitting across from me. Our eyes met, so I smiled at him and almost greeted him, but he barely responded: just a faint upturn of his mouth before turning his face away as if he didn't know me. Or maybe he did and preferred to pretend that he didn't remember me.

I quickly blinked my right eye to read his biodata. It read:

KAMEEL TAMIR TOOTNAJAN

25 YEARS

SINGLE

His name matched the Kameel that I knew, but his age was all wrong. Maybe he was lying about it, or maybe he was the grandson of the Kameel I knew. But the number of similarities between Kameel and this guy was uncanny: the same Armenian features and slim body type, the same old hairstyle; even his facial expressions and hand movements were those that used to set Kameel apart.

My feelings from that time came flooding back as if it were just yesterday.

I asked myself, "Why? Why Kameel? Why now?" My heartbeat began to race when I realized that day's date. It was as if time was lazy, unable to conjure up any new scenarios, so it resorted to replaying previous ones. A long time ago, on the 12th of June 2019 – the day I decided to openly admit to Zaid my no-child policy – Kameel appeared. In the same exact manner as today, the 12th of June, 2091.

Was it really a coincidence or some kind of omen? It was bizarre that both scenes matched up despite the extended time gap. Today, just like all those years ago, a mode of transport brought us together. On that day, our gazes had locked as we were standing face to face inside one of the Bus Rapid Transit vehicles. A woman left her seat when the bus stopped near the Sports City traffic circle. Kameel nodded at me to take her seat. He smiled and whispered, "Please, go on." I smiled back shyly, "Thank you, no, you," because I didn't know him at the time. While we dilly-dallied over the seat, some guy rushed from behind us and stole it. We looked at one another, clasping the iron pole between us, and laughed.

His presence was intriguing, a welcome answer to my search back then for something to distract me from thinking about how I would face Zaid that night. I was really tense and found chatting with Kameel a breath of fresh air. We had a quick chat, after which we exchanged phone numbers.

Kameel contacted me two days later. At that time, I was low after my split with Zaid. I was lost, hurting, feeling kind of betrayed at Zaid for abandoning me, and suffocating with guilt. I don't know if I was spurred on by my attraction to Kameel or by my need to flee from the mental state I found myself in. At first, I didn't think of what our encounters meant as much as how at ease I felt during them. But things between us heated up at an unnatural speed, and my feelings for Kameel grew intense.

Our rendezvous stretched on for two months, up until the day I found Zaid knocking on my door, confessing how he missed me and how he'd give up on having kids if it meant he could have me back in his life. His return hurt me somewhat, and my messy feelings for both men tormented me at that point in time; one of them loved me to the degree of denying himself, and the other caused a torrent of feelings I was unable to explain.

The kiss Kameel had planted on my lips the night before Zaid's return left me light-headed. His kiss was my forbidden fruit because I had been afraid of tasting it. I decided to run away from it and pretend it had never happened. That day I chose Zaid because I wasn't scared of loving him. I chose him because he didn't bring my being to a standstill. I chose him because he didn't stoke my desire to seize the wheel; instead he always reinforced my ability to steer calmly, wisely, deliberately. As time went on, I forgot Kameel and believed I was in the driver's seat when it came to my feelings. In times of joy, I felt at ease and admitted to myself that I had made the right choice. And in dark times, I berated myself for throwing my life away because I had been fearful of the unknown.

My feelings towards Kameel at that time now matched a great deal with my feelings towards life after death. I knew that both of these men could bring me indescribable joy, but I also knew that the price of that joy was my independence, my being, my existence. The feeling that drowned me in Kameel's presence scared me, and despite this feeling's force, it could just be a mere illusion. The brief scent of happiness that my soul inhaled was the whiff of a perfume eventually stolen away by the winds of reality, and by my need to cling to my roots firmly embedded in this world's soil.

Today, I felt the same need to distract myself from thinking about meeting Zaid. My feelings for Kameel surprised me after all these years, after he had faded from my memory. It was as if a dream was repeating itself, like it was a re-run on TV.

Was it logical for my mental state to be replicated in this way? And on the same date? On a similar mode of transport? With the very same person?

Could Kameel be some type of angel to whom the doors of heaven were opened from time to time so that he could materialize before me when my stress levels reached limits only he could quell? Or could he be a messenger that appeared to strengthen my resolve and stir in my heart the ability to make crazy decisions?

I hurried to speak to him as he was about to alight at the Al-Abdali metro stop. I approached him and called out "Kameel." He looked at me bowled over, before replying, "Janna?"

"That's right." I smiled and asked, "How are you?"

"Well, and you?"

I nearly added "long time no see," but caught myself because it was clear from his body language that he didn't know me. I apologized, "Sorry I thought you were someone I knew," but didn't add "a long time ago" because I was embarrassed to announce my real age in front of Kameel the grandson. I eased up when I remembered my biodata didn't show my age. But he surprised me when he quipped, "Even if you don't know me, I'd like to get to know you," grinning in a way that transported me back in time. It was a smile my heart knew well. My chest tightened.

He asked me if I was against him calling me later and setting up a get-together over coffee. I didn't have a problem with it now, just as I hadn't in the past. I told him I had to dash off to make it on time for my appointment at the office. After I left him, a strange headache imprinted with the past pounded against my temples as I faced again a period in my life I once thought had been folded up over time and buried.

I shot off to my office, fighting against thinking of the surreal scenario that my mind tried to draw up. My mind drew a link between Kameel's prophetic appearance and my feelings of my mother's closeness to me. I deduced from my constant sense of her presence that she agreed with my urge to bring her back to life. It felt as if she had conspired with Kameel and had sent him to me when she felt my need for him.

By the time I sent him on his way today, his appearance had helped me settle on coming clean with Zaid. In the past, his appearances had been a source of strength as I chose not to have children. Had Mom been planning for our future since that time?

Mom's disposition on the night after I had told Zaid my decision came back to me. Unlike her normal demeanor at that time – where she was no longer able to recognize me – she was calm and at peace. She had waited for me by the kitchen window. She looked at me affectionately when I went inside the house as if she was already in the know. She called out to me, asking why I was upset. I denied that anything was wrong. She came close and hugged me to her chest, letting me bawl. After I calmed down she whispered in my ear, "Let it be. Tears are good sometimes." Then, sighing, she quoted the Quran, "'It may be that you dislike a thing which is good for you.'[3] God has a plan for us all."

No sooner had she finished the sentence than the light

---

3 Surah Al-Baqarah (2:216)

went out from her eyes. I sighed. How quickly it went! A look of disorientation took its place, one that we had gotten used to seeing on her face. Flashes of awareness would appear at this stage of her Alzheimer's progression, making it seem as if her soul came and went from her body from time to time. Maybe those were the only moments where nerve impulses found a gateway to her recent memory, and returned her to who we knew her as... glimpses of hope that would revive us only to kill us with her when they faded.

Those moments of hope decreased over time, waning as the disease progressed. For me, the most crucial of those moments came *that* night, and although it might not have left an impression in her memory, it indelibly did on mine.

It was as if Mom came back to me today to assure me that I was in safe hands and what was happening in my life, the detestable things on the surface, would in the end give way to what was good for me. Her presence today was like that of my dream, and my feelings of her warm embrace on the day she comforted me after my breakup with Zaid was exactly what touched my heart when she called out to me in the dream: "I'm doing really well and I miss you. Come here so I can hug you."

Chapter 9

Destiny

SEEING Jihan behind the receptionist as I entered the newspaper office jolted me from my reverie. At first, I couldn't make her out when she started talking to me, but then I realized it was Jihan when I recalled her photo next to the article from that morning. Even though the picture as I remembered it appeared to exaggerate her hairstyle, looking at her in person convinced me that the photographer knowingly reduced the size of her hair in the picture as much as possible, because the area that her head occupied was enormous. She came across as a cartoon character, a blend of a lion's mane and a clown's body.

She greeted me enthusiastically, pouncing on me to embrace me. I was taken aback by her warmth and kindness, but I knew her well. Her kindness was usually just a cover for some need or the other that she was hiding. At this thought, I whispered to myself, "*God protect me.*"

"Janna, how are you, daarrling? Why do you look so run down?"

Even though I had known her for all these years, I was still caught off guard by her nasty remarks. I opened my mouth, taken aback and unable to respond at first.

"No, not tired or anything, actually it's the quite the opposite. I'm well rested today," I lied.

"Your eyes are a tad puffy. Maybe you didn't sleep well?"

"It's possible."

"Also why is your stomach swollen today? What did you have for dinner last night?" she chuckled as if she were teasing me. I almost took a cheap shot at her by calling her clown-like appearance and big mouth into question, but I regained my composure and kept tight-lipped.

"More importantly, Janna, are you all free tonight? I wanted to come visit Jamal. I want to speak to him about something."

"Sure, you can come over. What do you want to talk to him about?"

"About inheriting the birth-giving right after Jamal dies. You know the family's big and everyone'll be after this opportunity."

Hell-lady made her exit as I stood shell-shocked by her statement about settling the inheritance just like that, the audacity of it all, like it was some routine jaunt, and as if Jamal's life didn't mean a thing to her. Even though I had expected such a move from her, I felt a lump in my throat, deeply saddened because her words meant that the ramifications of Jamal's impending demise had truly transformed into a family feud before he had even passed on from this world. Maybe I'd have to back down from this battle out of reverence for Jamal in his final days. But I wasn't going to be able to bear his death without finding a stand-in for him. And I wasn't about to let Jihan rob me of this hope after she had kept Jamal from me for so many years back in the day.

How could she demand this right to procreate after she had left him high and dry during the hardest days of his life?

I got lost in her words and what they meant: the inevitability of confronting Zaid tonight about how I wanted to give birth to my mom. Her image from last night's dream came back to me and I felt a great yearning for it. I remembered Kameel's from this morning and wished I could call him and tell him of the madness that was my life.

I sat in my chair, trying to distract myself. I opened the newspaper's homepage on my e-lens and remembered Jihan's article. I projected in onto the office wall and zoomed in on the text.

DON'T KILL YOURSELVES FOR GOD HAS BEEN MERCIFUL TO YOU

Indeed God, mighty and majestic as He is, has generously blessed man and favored him over the rest of creation. As such we find that Islam has forbidden killing oneself and made it one of the gravest sins, only outweighed by the dire offense of shirk – equating something or someone else to almighty God. The beloved Prophet (peace be upon him) specified in his prophetic oral tradition – the hadith – transmitted by Al-Bukhari on the authority of Ibn Mas'ud (may God be pleased with him), three instances allowing the spilling of blood: justified revenge on a killer for his murder, punishing an adulterer (for marital betrayal), and killing an apostate of the religion to ward off unrest in the community. The Prophet said, "It isn't justified to let the blood of a Muslim fall, one that bears witness that there is no God but God and that I am His messenger except in one of the three cases: a murderer, an adulterous widow, and one who has left the religion."

In the past, humanity was under divine wisdom and will, standing helpless in front of the tyranny of old age and its power over the gradual end of human life. But God harnessed science and knowledge when there was good in it. Divine wisdom willed scientists studying humanity to explore the depth of the life code so they would find solutions to the numerous diseases we were powerless against in the past. The most important of these ailments was old age itself; that was and still is after the spread of its cure, considered among the leading causes of death.

No heavenly decree or national law globally (new or old) has ever encouraged man to surrender. And if in the past man kept death company because of old age, living with old age's difficulties and pains where there was no alternative, he has today pronounced his divorce from old age three times as the custom goes – all but erasing it from our dictionaries after triumphing over it and eliminating it as a threat.

We have to differentiate between the judiciary verdict of death and ruling of life, for life is in God's hands. He who has the ability to grant human life has the ability to take it away when He pleases. With the availability of the ageing cure today, refusing the cure or denying its existence should be considered a type of suicide and an open challenge to divine will.

It is up to the government to expedite ratifying the necessary legislation and presenting it to Parliament as soon as possible. Suicide has never been legislated for or against, and so it falls upon us to fill this legal gap, so to say, and enact a law that corresponds *with the zeitgeist.*

From an economic standpoint the health ministry's official report published yesterday brings to light the growing cost of old age and its annual cost to the national economy, a whopping 370 million dinars. Furthermore, the report indicates that not only is it one of the leading causes of death but also one of the biggest factors contributing to poverty all over the Hashemite kingdom. The elderly as we know are unable to participate in generating wealth.

In closing, I leave you to ruminate on this hadith transmitted by Abu Hurayra, may God be pleased with him: "He who falls from a mountain to kill himself is in Hellfire and will keep falling in Hell over and over, forever and eternally, and he who sips poison to kill himself will sip it in Hell over and over, forever and eternally, and he who kills himself with a steel weapon will have that weapon in hand, thrusting it into his stomach in Hell over and over, forever and eternally."

- Jihan Awad

What an instigator Jihan was, playing on people's religious leanings in order to please her higher-ups at work! I understood the angle that she started off from, making correlations between refusing the golden pill and suicide, but I saw it as a different type of suicide. You could not classify it in the same category as killing oneself.

If one gave in to the argument that old age is an illness harming man, then this illness must be a part of his genetic makeup that he's born with. The choice was to cheat nature by extending human life, and though it is a choice I supported myself, religious clerics had opposed it in the past, as it entailed tampering with our genetic code.

Today, science had reached the stage where it gave man the ability to lengthen his life. This, in my opinion, was a personal choice, an individual right; the state had no right to steal it from him. Those who "sold" religion might doctor ideas to influence the layman to bypass government policies. But I refused to touch one of man's basic rights, especially his right to choose between life and death.

If we refused the legalization of suicide in the past, even with the limitations of human life that were then inescapable, then this refusal did not apply today, when man's lifespan was no longer limited.

Someday, science might lead us to edit genetic material to the extent that growing old would no longer be a part of life's equation. But, today, we were far from that and we had to defend the individual's right to choose whether to take the eternal youth pill until we came to the time where old age was no longer considered a natural choice.

I really had to prepare a suitable riposte that encompassed all these thoughts of mine, and publish it in the same column of the newspaper, pronto.

CHAPTER 10

ZAID'S SURPRISE

TIME is like a magnet with poles, focal points that have the power to attract events and collect these events around them. Far from these poles, in areas where the magnetic pull is weaker, the tempo of events slows down and time stretches out painfully, interminably long. In this manner did the hours crawl by at the office from morning until I had to head home. Long hours, eventless, but crammed with tension between the two poles of time: Zaid's voice like a broken record ("I also have something I want to talk to you about"), and the image of him preoccupied with unloading whatever was on his mind.

I couldn't believe what my ears were relaying to me as they carried Zaid's words up to my brain. I was sitting across from him on a terrace of one of the Italian restaurants between the skyscrapers in Abdali. Each of us was wound up, each one harboring a secret, akin to a surgical scalpel dissecting our relationship only to put it back together. We'd either repair our relationship or screw it up further, I didn't know, but both of us were certain that we were no longer strong enough to keep on going with the way things were.

What he was about to reveal to me paralyzed my thoughts; on the other hand I couldn't gauge the effect of what he was about to propose on what I was going to disclose to him!

Was I wrong to give him the opportunity to speak first? Would his news be wilder than my wish to give birth to my mother, making me come across as more rational than him?

"What do you think?" he asked me when he was done talking. I was quiet, awkward, as he looked into my eyes, a look that bore much expectation.

Usually I thought I was the wacky one in the relationship, but today I was convinced that I had finally passed on the baton of craziness to Zaid. If it were a different time and if the situation were less high-stakes, I would have patted myself on the back and proudly congratulated myself.

But the comedy of what he was proposing was nothing for me to be proud of, because it was wrapped up in the tragedy of the truth. Zaid's words weren't in a faraway dream, but they conveyed a decision that meant the end of my life as I knew it with him. Even though I had expected him to leave me, I just hadn't pictured it in this way.

I let him speak at length with faltering words, which were dominated by great pauses of silence.

"Janna you know I've been depressed for a while now... I'm not happy with my life. The only time I remember being truly happy was during my adolescent years. I want to relive those days... I want to go back to my childhood. A lot of people are literally reliving their childhood these days. I just want to go back to when I was an adolescent, ten years old.

How many years will you be able to put up with me until I grow up?"

I took a deep breath so that I wouldn't react aggressively. I couldn't refuse him at a time when I myself was gearing up to ask him something even more difficult. But I couldn't believe this is what he wanted.

I tried to delay my response. "Listen, Zaid," I finally said, "returning to one's childhood is a Christian fad. One that's spread among fundamentalist Christian groups that read the Biblical verse literally, that 'If you don't become as children, you won't enter heaven.' If you come at it from an Islamic perspective, the age of a human in heaven is 33 years. Meaning pretty much the youthful age that we're living now, thanks to the pill."

"It's not about it being a Muslim or Christian issue, Janna! I'm suffocating, I need a change in my life. Maybe this adventure will pull me out of my depression. Maybe adolescence will help me regain my zest and love for life," he said, and then added hesitantly, "Essa also decided to do the same thing. But he'll stay a child forever. He said the end of the world is approaching and that he as a Christian believes that the only way to the heavenly kingdom is to go back to being a child like you said." He sighed and then continued, "Oh God, imagine if Essa and I went back to those days! We'd go back to playing in the neighborhood, carefree. We'd chase after each other. We'd play marbles, tag, and play hide-and-seek. We'd go back to school and make new friends." He chuckled and added, "I swear I'll be a good kid. I won't annoy you. Mom always said I had a good head on my shoulders as a kid, so don't you worry."

I cut in, irritated, "Zaid, Zaid, Zaid, why are you getting carried away? Yes, you can reprogram your body cells and shrink your body physically. You can also slightly dull your mental capabilities to resemble that of an adolescent. But overall, you know only so well that you cannot get rid of your awareness, knowledge, and social maturity. You'll be yourself in a child's body. Nothing will change except for your physical structure." Taking another deep breath, I warned him, "Don't think you're going to be like the participants in yesterday's reality show. They're going back to the first day of their lives. They're going to have their entire memories wiped clean. Meaning they're actually going to be kids. They're going the whole way, not halfway."

I was hoping to convince him with logic, to make clear the reality of his decision to him, but I was actually pondering what this decision meant for me and what this "adventure" meant for our relationship.

At that moment I remembered Kameel, and felt ashamed of myself for doing so. I tried to keep from broaching the nature of my relationship with Zaid, but failed. We'd lost intimacy for some years now, just as we had lost it several times past in our relationship. As usual, it was a silent decision from both sides. We'd agreed on being courteous to one another after having lost the pleasure of bodily closeness. We had distanced ourselves from one another physically and emotionally. We ended up preferring a fraternal relationship, because of which we couldn't talk about how our relationship had changed, that we had ignored it, and how we were now clinging onto to a shadow of its former self. We believed our long years of companionship held more importance for our marital relationship than any performance in the bedroom. Thus, even though I knew Zaid the child wouldn't approach me emotionally any differently from Zaid the man, I found myself questioning him: "So then, what do you think our relationship is going to be like?"

He looked at me stupefied. Maybe he was trying to confirm that I actually wanted to go *there*. He got a grip and calmly responded, "Janna, I won't deny that there's a problem in how we relate to one another sexually. Maybe part of the problem is that I've even stopped thinking about it. And maybe at this stage we actually need a change like this."

"Maybe you're right," I answered as I tried to push away any remnant of the feelings that Kameel had aroused inside of me this morning.

"You don't have to give me an answer now. Think about it and let me know." He straightened up, adjusted his position, before startling me slightly when he said, "Now it's your turn. What did you want to talk to me about?"

At the moment that he uttered the question, my watch lit up announcing a message in my inbox. Kameel's face flashed on the screen fleetingly before it disappeared to be replaced by the number one next to the unread notification icon. I hastily blinked my eye to read the message before getting back to Zaid.

Janna, I'm stoked that I got to know you this morning. You up for a cup of coffee tomorrow?

I ignored Kameel's message and started to lay bare to Zaid

what was going on inside of me. My words also faltered and were dominated by intervals of silence. "Zaid, like you, I've been depressed for a while. To tell you the truth, I'm scared. Scared of losing Jamal. No one else from my family will be alive when he goes."

I felt short of breath while talking about Jamal's departure. Just thinking about it increased my anxiety. I tried in vain to rein in my tears, but Zaid's gentleness and the warmth of his touch as his hand patted my arm made it easier for them to fall. He looked at me compassionately and quickly cut me off: "I'm your family, Janna. I've always been and always will be."

I almost shot back by reminding him of what he had just said. How could he be my family and be dreaming up ways to run away from me? And how could I guarantee having him by my side when there was an inclination deep down to kick him out of my life? He no doubt had always been my support and help over the years. He was the rock that I leaned on and the embrace that I warmed my face in. He was my husband, my friend, and my brother. Because of this I found myself unable to understand my aversion to his existence, or my inclination to his replace him.

Maybe those feelings that pushed me away from him were what increased my fear of being alone, my latching on-to Jamal's existence and my dream of bringing Mom back. "Once I was watching this talk show host interview an Egyptian actress – I forget her name. The host asked her about how her mother's death had affected her. You know what she told him?"

"What?"

"She told him that her mother hadn't died and that she was still very much alive with her. She said it's impossible for a daughter to believe that her mother is dead, no matter how much time has passed. And I, after all these years, I can't believe Mom's dead and gone. I dreamed last night," I smiled as I went on, "a strange dream. I'm not sure how to explain it. She told me that she's fine and missing me. I also miss her. A lot. Let me confess something. I asked a specialist – Mom's genetic code exists; it's really straightforward to implant it into a cell and culture it into a fetus. I know I have always been against getting pregnant. And I know I've done you wrong. It's just that, if Jamal goes, Mom has to come back. The cell can be implanted in my womb..." I ended the last sentence whispering, "... and Mom will be back in my life."

CHAPTER 11

A DIFFERENT KIND OF INHERITANCE

I T'S ironic that I feel just as horrible when I hurt someone as when they hurt me. In those situations where I've
been forced to hurt, knowingly and with prior planning,
someone I love in order to get back at a third party who has
wronged me, my anguish has been by far greater than if I were
retaliating against a direct perpetrator of my misery.

I acted out of character as I weighed my desire to give
birth to Mom against Zaid's wish to return to childhood. I
regretted what I did because I didn't like the idea of exchanging benefits in a marital relationship in this way. Zaid and I
had gotten used to giving to each other freely. Giving ruled by
the mutual unspoken understanding of each of our duties to
provide comfort and happiness for our life partner.

I was ashamed of myself when Zaid caught me off guard
with the amount of grace with which he dealt with the issue.
Yes, he didn't hesitate to confirm that carrying my mother's
genetic code didn't mean bringing her back to life, but instead
it meant giving birth to a new person who would carry her

genes, though with a different consciousness and soul. It was just like how I didn't shy away from reminding him that his return to childhood wouldn't bring back the past that he had lived or the happiness he was hoping for. But in the end, he asserted that his standing by me and supporting me in fulfilling my desire would not depend on my assent to what he wanted. He also put me at ease when he clarified that he no longer dreamed of a child bearing his name at a time when his life on earth was no longer limited as it had been before, and that his sole wish now was to beat a retreat from the world of adults and sail away to the world of childhood.

It seemed to me that a streak of insanity had struck us both, a strange desire pushing each of us to escape the rut our relationship was stuck in. I dared to explain to him that to make my dream come true, Jamal would need to be convinced to bequeath me the birth-giving right which the family had claim to after his death. I told him how Jihan had stunned me that very morning by wanting to settle the matter in favor of herself and her children. I drew his attention to the article she had written, and made clear to him the contradiction between what she was calling for in the article and what she was practicing in reality. I told him how she was only looking out for her narrow-minded interests without thinking about the consequences of her actions. I was convinced she wrote the article to get into her superiors' good books, without giving a thought to the fallout in the lives of people around her. I spelled it out for him that maybe she hadn't actually thought about what the law meant to her and its effect on the birth-giving right that she was angling for, if the law were applied immediately, and that it was likely both the law and Jamal were the least of her concerns as she didn't understand anything except her selfish needs, and couldn't see past her own nose.

Zaid inquired if Jamal had read the article and I replied in the negative. I told him how I'd wiped it from the house's network so he wouldn't read it and get upset. He respected my wishes to shelter Jamal but found the article a chance to get back at Jihan and make things go my way. He suggested I show Jamal the article right away, before Jihan arrived that night.

I hesitated. How could I take part in depressing one of my nearest and dearest, in his time of weakness? But I stayed silent and agreed grudgingly, as Jihan had left me no choice, and time was, as usual, far from being on my side.

It was a desperate attempt, of which I foreknew the result. Jihan's bewitchment of Jamal was iron-clad, withstanding my meddling interference. He was able to forgive and vindicate her no matter how much she hurt him or did him wrong. And tonight was no different, despite Zaid's close reading of the article to Jamal and his rereading of the inflammatory sentences in it over and over: "It is up to the government to expedite ratifying the necessary legislation and presenting it to Parliament as soon as possible"; "Suicide has never been legislated for or against, and so it falls upon us to fill this legal gap…"; and so on. However, Jamal's shock at these snippets lasted only a few minutes; so did his censure of Jihan's gall. His misery transformed into joy the moment Zaid informed him that Jihan wanted to pay him a visit.

His happiness at seeing her didn't incense me this time

because I couldn't bear seeing him unhappy, especially if I was the reason for it. But I did get irked the instant my eyes fell on Jihan and Khalid right behind her.

I should have expected her to bring him because this whole situation was a family matter, after all.

Her hair wasn't styled to the same degree it had been this morning, but she seemed taller wearing those sky-high red heels. She closed in on me, leaning over to kiss me as if we were the best of friends or hadn't just seen each other at the office a few hours earlier. Then, leaving me, she made a beeline for Jamal's room. I followed her, looking intently at her as she waddled into Jamal's in those heels, tight jeans, and see-through shirt.

She approached him and – very much out of character – kissed his head. She asked about his health, and then sat down on a seat next to his bed, joking with him, "What, you haven't changed your mind about dying yet?" He nodded, a wan smile flitting across his lips.

For a moment I mulled over Jihan's insinuation that she wanted Jamal to keep on living, realizing that though they might just be meaningless words, they were guaranteed to stoke Jamal's will to live on, even if for a few more years. I retired to the kitchen for a couple of minutes to make some coffee.

When I returned, Jihan had adjusted her position, her back straight with one leg draped over the other. She took a cup of coffee from my hand, sipped it, and placed it on the small table in front of her. Then she said in an ultra-formal tone, "Jamal, since you're so insistent on dying, we have to discuss the issue of inheritance."

Her gaze shifted from Jamal to Khalid to Zaid before it settled on me. She continued, "Janna, Jamal, I'm sorry. Don't get upset with me, but one just *has* to be practical in these circumstances. I'm not talking about financial inheritance... financial rights are clearly outlined in the law." She focused her gaze on Jamal and went on in the same tone, "I'm talking about the family's chance to inherit your birth-giving right."

My heart raced, anxious about the effect of her words on him. I had every intention of interrupting her, but she didn't leave me any leeway. I stepped towards him and patted his shoulder while she continued, "Every day we're hearing about family feuds over this very issue. The norm, as you all know, is for the first-born son to inherit it. Khalid and I have discussed the matter, and we've decided that since I'm still alive, and after Jamal goes I'll be the eldest, the best thing is for the birth-giving right to be in my hands."

My eyebrows shot up involuntarily as she repeated her position as the presumptive eldest member of the family, shooting a cursory glance at me as she did so, but I didn't comment. Actually, not a single one of us opened our mouths: Khalid, her supporter, whom she had convinced of her intentions before she had come over; Jamal, the helpless one in the face of her opinions and desires from the very moment he met her; Zaid, who didn't have the guts to intervene in a family matter in which he had no stake; and I, who had fled from confrontation on a matter that was sacred to me, fearful that the discussion would take an ugly turn that would worry Jamal and distress him further in his final days.

Jihan exploited our silence and dared to take out a file from her bag. She put it on the table in front of her and continued: "I spoke with my lawyer and he's prepared this will for me. Jamal, all you have to do is write the name of the beneficiary in this blank space here, and sign at the end with today's date." She picked up a handful of *mlabbis* – sugar-coated almonds – and popped them into her mouth, adding as she chewed with graceless relish, "You don't have to sign now. Tomorrow I'll swing by in the evening and pick it up then."

Jihan didn't draw out her visit. She left after accomplishing her mission. I walked her and Khalid to the front door and coldly said goodbye. Then I went back to Jamal's room. I sat beside him on the bed, kissed his forehead and whispered, "Don't you worry now, you know her, she's always been like that." He smiled meekly but said nothing.

I clasped his hand and kissed it. I put it on my face and looked to the right, to a picture of Mom on his bedside table. I heaved a sigh before cautiously saying, "Jamal, you know where the word '*Akh*,' brother, came from? Mom always said it came from 'Argh,' meaning pain, because there's no one in the world who can ease your pain like your brother." I pressed on his hand as I tried to drain the emotion from my voice, and asked him jokingly, "After you're gone, who am I going to say '*Argh*' to?"

I forced a laugh as I carried on, "You remember when you were a kid and Mom bought you that toy car? You loved it so much, to the point where after you saw the funeral of some musician on TV, you started begging Mom to bury your car with you when you died. Mom got ticked off at you and said

'God forbid' and told you not to say that. And I, being just a little girl, said to her, 'Don't say "God forbid."'" What's wrong with it, if the one who's dying is going back to God?"

I laced my fingers with his and passed my left hand gently over his feeble forearm. Using my index finder, I concealed that red light on his wrist bracelet that read his vital signs, indicating that his days were numbered. I leaned my head on his shoulder and said, "Now you're getting ready to go, and every day I tell myself, God forbid, God forbid, God forbid."

He lay still next to me, as if he hadn't heard me. Between consciousness and unconsciousness, I heard him say in a faltering voice, barely audible from his throat, "Janna, open the door, Mom and Dad have come to get me."

How I wished that their presence were real, that I could rush to the door, open it, and throw myself into their embrace. I would grab them and beg them to take not only Jamal. My spirit would leave my body and kiss their feet. I would beg their souls to take me with them wherever they were headed.

But he was hallucinating. And I was too. Shortly after, the look in his eyes changed and he came back to reality. He asked for a glass of water. I hurried to get it for him. When I came back, his forehead was drenched in sweat. I wiped it and moistened his face with a wet cloth. I felt him regain his energy, and sat down facing him, saying, "Me too, Mom also visited me last night. She told me she's fine and that she misses you," I lied. "Tomorrow you'll be together up there. If everything goes well, promise me you'll come back to get me," I said playfully. He smiled, nodding his head.

"Promise me," I insisted.

"I promise," he said feebly.

"Jamal, can I ask you for one last thing?"

He bobbed his head once more waiting to hear my request, but I realized I wasn't up to saying it. I choked, wracked by the feeling that my soul would rather leave my body than hear me ask Jamal to inherit his right to procreation.

I wiped my tears. I closed my eyes. I pinched my nose and took a deep breath. I regained my composure and whispered, "It's a tall order. I can't say it. It's not coming out." I clasped his hands and kissed them twice, thrice, four times until I gained the courage to say, "I want your right to bring new life to replace you, Jamal, after you've passed on. I want to give birth. I want someone to compensate me for losing you."

CHAPTER 12

SPIRITUAL GATEKEEPER

I WAS hungry. I felt heaviness in my stomach and a jolting pain in my lower back. I moved stealthily as I searched for food in the family kitchen. I opened the fridge and took a look inside. I found it dark, with near-empty shelves. On the right, were three eggs, one of them cracked, the inside goop splattered across the shelf. It smelled horrendous, making me nauseous. I coughed. The first shelf in front of me was empty, and on the second were two unripe onions next to a plate of uncovered hummus, now inedible. I grabbed the two green onions and shut the fridge door. I turned to the right. The frypan on the stove was crusty, with the dregs of fried onions stuck to it. I stepped towards the pan and picked up the cover of the pot next to it, only to find some tomato soup, barely enough to fill a coffee cup. I put the cover back and turned left to the bag of bread flung on the tile floor. I went towards it and preoccupied myself with opening it when I heard Mom say, "This onion here is for Jamal; don't you go eating it."

Her sudden appearance jolted me, but, despite my hunger, her words didn't irk me. It was as if she were pointing out my error, so I corrected myself. How could I eat Jamal's onion? This onion that was meant for him, meaning he was to die, not me.

She was sitting, head bent over, in the sitting room absorbed in designing a new painting whose features I didn't recognize. To me she seemed psychologically and physically relaxed, a halo of calmness atop her head, her mien ethereal.

I left her and entered Jamal's room. In stark contrast to Mom, he was worn out, splayed across the bed, tired, feverish, his forehead pouring with sweat. His body was adolescent-like, reminding me of when he was younger. But in spite of how young he looked, I knew he was on his deathbed. I gave him the onion and said, "This onion's for you, from Mom."

He took it and hungrily scarfed a chunk down. After he swallowed, he closed his eyes and surrendered his soul. At that moment I felt his spirit fall on me, and I felt the fetus kick furiously within me, hurting me.

I woke up, tired, dripping with sweat, hungry. I felt my stomach, confused about what the dream meant. In the past I used to observe the harmony of death and life in the families around me. Usually I would see it as a coincidence when a new birth came to a family with the passing of an aged person; a seemingly natural way to bring grandchildren to life at a time when their grandparents were approaching death. With the changing of time and life itself, the situation became clearer. Today, families hurry to replace individuals they lose, as if there is a fine thread running between the one that is being lost and the one that is arriving. Obscure signs are entrenched in Buddhist philosophy around the principle of reincarnating souls. As if the departing souls swim in a back room, standing in a line, waiting, each eager to grab the chance of a rebirth to return to the world.

My dream transformed how I viewed my womb: from being a mere tool for birth to a spiritual gatekeeper bringing back to the world the souls that it had lost. I felt myself bearing the responsibility to bring back my family members one by one, if fate looked favorably on me. I hoped my first birth would be Mom, whom I adored. My beloved Dad, Mueen, would be second. My last child, who would be spoilt to the hilt, would be my brother, my partner in crime: Jamal.

CHAPTER 13

LIFE FROM THE WOMB OF DEATH

I REMEMBERED that Kameel had invited me for a cup of coffee that morning. I tossed and turned in my bed because I wasn't ready to get up yet, but thinking about meeting Kameel slightly rejuvenated me. I looked at my watch: 9 a.m. Our rendezvous was in an hour, but I wasn't about to leave Jamal today after his wristband had indicated a worsening of his vital signs – he was in a critical state. Because of this, I had already toyed with the idea of asking Kameel to come over to the house instead.

He came right on time, looking as handsome as his grandfather. He wore a white shirt with faded blue stripes, taking me back to what his grandfather used to wear long ago. He had rolled up the sleeves around his forearms exactly as his grandfather used to, as if he had inherited even the simplest of his habits along with his genetic code. I greeted him like we had known each other for ages, hugging him, pecking his cheek, and beckoning him into the living room.

They say that every person has a distinctive bodily scent

that interacts in a unique way with the cologne that he wears, but the fragrance of Yves St Laurent was indiscernible between grandfather and grandson, the scent was one and the same, the cologne the same. So was the attraction.

"Sorry for changing the venue. I couldn't get up and leave Jamal on his own."

"No worries. What's more important is, how is he? Tired?"

"In the middle of last night, he had a minor stroke. He woke up drained, unable to even recite the alphabet. Most likely these strokes will increase rapidly from here on out." I felt tense, so I suggested, "Would you like to sit in the garden?"

We moved to sit outside. On our way, I commented in a way that I hoped came across as spontaneous, "Actually, you know what, you're a carbon copy of your grandfather." He grinned and nodded his head in agreement. "Everyone says that to me even though I don't really remember him."

But I do, very well, I repeated in my head but said aloud, "God bless his soul, when did he pass?"

"In June, 2052. He suffered a stroke at one of Sabuha's concerts in Jerash." I almost fell down the three steps leading to the entrance of the garden. I lost my balance when I recalled the crowd gathered that day to the right of the amphitheater. They said someone had suffered a stroke. There was a yell followed by wailing. At that moment, I grabbed Zaid's arm and told him to take me away from the scene of the incident. I didn't know then that it was Kameel, which is why I rushed to ignore what had happened, as it didn't concern me. I let Jihan hustle us through to get to Sabah for a photo op with her before she left for the amphitheater.

We were flabbergasted at the renewal of her youth at a time when the treatment for old age was still monopolized by the elite. If Kameel had had the money back then to access the treatment, maybe his arteries could have been renewed, allowing him to sidestep that stroke and be sitting here with us now, sipping coffee.

I felt his presence as his grandson pulled the rattan chair towards the shade of the fig tree, inquiring, "How did you know him?"

I smiled. "Like I got to know you, while travelling by public transport." I carried the table and placed it down between the two chairs.

"How do you like your coffee? Sweet like he did?"

I turned to the large fan in the garden that sensed our presence and automatically turned on to dampen the searing morning heat. I left to get the coffee and returned after a few minutes. I gave it to him with a piece of *ma'moul* – date filled pastry – as I repeated, "The resemblance is uncanny, it's like you two are the same person."

He responded, "I still can't take it in that you're from my grandfather's generation. You don't look it at all."

"These days no one is defined by age. We've all become one generation," I offered.

"But there are folks you can pick out based on their clothes, the way they talk, or their mannerisms. Though everyone is biologically similar, it's like every generation has its own culture, thoughts, customs, and traditions."

I remembered my snail-like movement that carried on for years during my second round of youth. It was as if I was still living in my old body, cautious when walking, careful when sitting or leaning over, afraid that any sudden movement could break a fragile bone or rip a weak tendon. I strove to get rid of my sluggishness and, though I succeeded, I never regained the foolhardiness of my original youth. I no longer cut my finger by mistake when chopping veggies for cooking; I no longer crash into a crystal-clear glass door in haste; I no longer leave the house only to remember I've left my sunglasses behind; and I also no longer stumble when walking except on rare occasions like what just happened. The credit could be due to the maturity of my consciousness or my getting used to steering clear of those simple things that with time I came to identify as potholes, through trial and error.

But frankly I think he was buttering me up when he said that my appearance didn't correlate with my generation, as I still dressed the same way: faded colors and clothing of a relaxed fit were my thing. I liked a particular way of dressing and I bought my clothes from stores for those of my age group. I tried to remain as contemporary as possible, following the latest fashion trends and selecting from its oeuvre whatever suited my taste and vision of self.

His words made me review what I was wearing: a baggy white blouse streaked with black lines, loose brown pants. Before he arrived, I thought they were a good choice for a cup of coffee at home with a "stranger," but now I wondered if what I chose really showcased the generation to which I belong. What did it matter even if it did? It's funny that our culture still prefers youth even though age is no longer an indication of less vitality.

"You're right, Kameel. I think that the days of someone's first round of youth has a large impact on determining his choices and interests later on in life. Obviously, every generation will be affected by the prevailing culture. You know, I really envy your generation."

He looked at me, startled. "Why?" he asked.

"Because you're all lucky, being born in a time where the cure for old age exists. You're not obsessed with age and time like we were. There's no fear of growing old, of sickness, that you have a limited time to achieve something – a degree in your early twenties, marriage and an apartment before you're thirty, and having kids before the grim reaper steals you away. Funnily enough, we entertain ourselves with our children, only to wake up a few years later realizing that we've lost our youth, our bodies old and fragile, every part in pain, not working as they used to." I laughed and continued, "There's no such a thing as the grim reaper anymore, I guess. Time has put him out of business, not like how it was for us back in the day."

"Obviously life is different today, but I'm also envious of your generation. You guys have the advantage of time on your side. Someone like me requires years of work to be able to achieve a fraction of what you've achieved in your career. Look at the standout names in the world of journalism and media today. The overwhelming majority is from the first generation. Not just that, the owners of capital, land, apartments, and companies as well as those in the upper echelons of society… everything. You guys didn't leave anything for us."

I remembered our encounter the previous day on the metro when he said my name. I thought at that time that he knew me from my electronic biodata but it seems that he already knew me and had been following my articles and journalistic achievements. He went on, "There's a huge imbalance in the scale of power between the generations. Your generation just keeps on hogging all the wealth, not even giving us a chance."

"In our time, one would bequeath his wealth to his children when he died, divide and distribute it among the generation after him. But now life is something else. He who doesn't die, doesn't bequeath," I opined as I picked up Abla, my cat, and put her in my lap. "Have you met my cutie Abla?"

He stretched out his hand to stroke the cat. "Awww, my God, what beautiful blue eyes! Gorgeous! Persian?"

"Yes, Persian. If only you'd seen her when she was a kitten. She was cuter, smaller, and more energetic. Now she's become a teddy bear you move from one place to the next, sleeping the whole day."

He pulled her out from my hands and placed her on his lap, and started petting her. "She's gotten old, poor thing. How old is she? Fourteen, fifteen?"

"Fourteen."

"You haven't thought of renewing her youth?"

"I've been thinking about it, even though I'm not that convinced about the renewal of an animal's youth at a time when a lot of people are still unable to renew their own. I'm really attached to her though, and I need her more and more these days." I sat quietly, thinking of the excuse I'd just given him. To be honest, a part of me linked her life to Jamal's. I told myself if Jamal wanted to stay, I would have renewed her youth in a heartbeat.

"You know, Kameel, maybe the thing you should feel most grateful for is that you were born in a time that relieves you from feelings of pain and loss. Death was bitterly tangible for us in the past. With each scientific discovery we would push it a little further away. Mankind never imagined that he'd be able to cheat death in this way." I moved my hand to shoo away a fly that had settled on the coffee cup, looked up at the azure sky, and then to the trees around us. I stretched out my arm and picked a flower from the jasmine bush behind us, brought it next to my nose, inhaled its sweet aroma, and continued, "As if it's magic. Sometimes I feel as if I'm living in a dream, as if we're in heaven." Sighing, I added, "But the lifespan of this dream has yet to be traversed, it won't ever end." I fell silent for a moment, and afterwards said, "A long time ago, my great dream in life was to see Mom and Dad living out their youth. To see them in good health and spirits, without any sickness, old age, or pain."

Hell-lady's voice wafted in from the footpath next to the garden, interrupting us suddenly: "Janna, Janna!" It was as if she had been spying on me while I sat with Kameel. She called out my name again, made her way to the garden gate, opened it, and came towards us.

I got up to greet her, "Jihan, umm, hi. How are you? Come have a seat."

"I'm good. I came by to give something to Khalid and thought I should greet you before I go to the office."

"Yes, come, sit and have a cup of coffee with us."

"No, it's fine. I'm in a hurry. How's Jamal today? Did he sign the will?"

"Jamal's really exhausted. I don't think he'll make it through the day."

I ignored her question about the will. She appeared moved, came closer, and hugged me.

"I'm sorry, darling." As she let go of me, she added, "Just make sure he signs the will before anything happens to him. We'll be in a pickle if you don't."

As if she had abruptly become aware of Kameel's presence, she didn't wait for an answer from me; she looked at him instead and said, "Pardon me." She approached him and stretched out her hand, introducing herself, "I'm Jihan Awad, famous writer." She scrutinized him as if she were trying to make sense of something obscure yet related that had surfaced in her memory. "Your face is familiar. We've met before, right?" Her memory didn't take more than a moment to bring up a clear picture from the past. She laughed, proud of herself, and added heartily, "Ah, I've got it, you used be in love with Janna way back!"

She might as well have slapped me across the face; her audacity shocked me. My eyes bulged but I quickly calmed myself. I tried to hide my embarrassment by saying, "Jihan this is Kameel's grandson, not the Kameel that you know."

She looked at him, top to bottom, making sure for herself. "Okay, anyway, let me be on my way, I'm late for work. Finish your coffee before it gets cold." With the corners of her mouth upturned, she winked at me on her way out, as if she already knew how I felt about Kameel.

"Jihan was married to Jamal." I informed Kameel. "We've gotten used to her behavior; it seems her whole life she has spoken before she has thought something through. More importantly, what were we talking about?"

"About dreams." He was looking at me differently now, as if what Jihan had said to him had reassured him in some way. It confirmed for him that his feelings for me matched mine for him. We didn't need to talk about it, maybe because language did not possess the *mots justes* for the bond that tied Kameel to me. It wouldn't do this bond justice to say that it was a type of love, or sexual attraction, or spiritual connection. The most important characteristic for this bond was that it was unclear to reason, fiendishly difficult to categorize it in a specific framework, but at the same time as clear as day to the heart. How could it not be when my feelings for Kameel filled my heart with peace?

The beeping of my watch alerting us that Jamal was suffering a more violent stroke cut short this short-lived peace. Kameel and I rushed into his bedroom. I knew for sure then that his time had come. I stood calmly at his bedside, completely surrendering to destiny. My calmness at that moment was atypical. There was no fear, apprehension, or even sadness. In fact, it was the opposite: I felt an unexpected internal peace. A peace whose source – whether it was from Jamal's peaceful face that was glowing even more now, or Kameel's comforting embrace, or the failing of my brain to work when faced with such a terrifying moment – I couldn't pinpoint.

For the first time in my life, I felt tears devoid of sentiment fall down my cheeks. Kameel's presence at that moment proved to me that he was sent straight to me from heaven. And just like in the dream, I felt my hands move towards my midriff to feel my stomach, while my soul yelled out, calling for my mother.

CHAPTER 14

PERSONAL FREEDOMS?

THE RIGHT TO CHOOSE BETWEEN LIFE AND DEATH

My brother Jamal was a devout Muslim throughout his lifetime. Neither prayer nor the opportunity to fast escaped him, even in his final days when his weakness escalated and the power of old age completely overpowered him, leaving him with dry joints that paralyzed his movement. I would see him battle his body and make it obey as much as he could in order to perform his religious duties and put his conscience at ease. I saw him hide his pain as he prostrated time after time to offer his prayers, challenging the worsening inflammation in his joints. And when he was no longer able to genuflect, he started offering the entirety of his prayers standing up. And when his feet were unable to carry him, he would say his prayers sitting down, weighed down by guilt. In his last days he would pray lying down on his back or lying on his side, gesturing with his head and eyes the act of prostration itself, an act he longed to perform.

Despite a joint inflammation treatment that would have re-

juvenated his joints being available on the market for a long time,
he refused to have any pill that would prevent the natural aging
of his body. He believed that his fate was written in his genetic
code and that the time of his departure was determined from the
moment he was born. He persevered and endured, was in agony
and struggled. He witnessed the decline of his strength and emaci-
ation of his body with grace at a time when everyone around him
was racing to turn back the clock to go back to their prime! He was
God-fearing and lived a powerful life, smiling till his last moment
of consciousness, looking forward to the moment when he'd meet
his Maker, looking forward to a time of immortality in his final
resting place, hoping for heaven.

Last week, before Jamal left this world, he was overcome with
fear. His fear didn't stem from his approaching hour, but from one
of his dreams being snatched away by Parliament, which is plan-
ning to pass a law to ban suicide. He left us terrified that one of his
most basic human rights would be wrested from him, the right to
choose between life and death. He left us, beseeching me to contest
this unjust law.

Twenty years ago, before the spread of the rejuvenation pill,
old age was a part of the natural life equation for us humans. At
that time, thanks to steady technological advancement, mankind
could eliminate and restrict the proliferation of all infectious dis-
eases that had led to the destruction of human life in the ages that
came before. With the spread of social welfare, the supply of food
in unprecedented quantities, the increasing interest in health and
fitness, the number of middle-aged humans tripled within a cen-
tury. This was a natural increase in the middle-aged demographic
without any doctoring of the basic cell structure. As for today, the

new, smart nanobots work on a cellular level to clean them continually of the offscourings of biological processes. This technological process is outside of the natural framework that was created for the human body.

All of us know of Jamal's great contribution to biotechnology. He was the first to develop the vaccine against Alzheimer's, spurred on by his aspiration – which was never fulfilled – to save my mother from the grip of this disease. His contributions to stem cell research played a role in treating numerous illnesses that accompany old age, including Parkinson's and diabetes. There isn't enough space here to mention all of Jamal's professional achievements, as his history is replete with them, but what I have mentioned has only been to draw attention to how Jamal wasn't looking for immortality through his work; instead his aim was to strengthen man and provide him with some type of ability to choose. It never occurred to him that one day his medical accomplishments would transform death from the inevitable to an unfulfilled hope.

Far from the religious problem of explaining Quranic verses and the honorable prophet's sayings in light of life today, and contrary to my personal position of choosing everlasting youth and hanging onto this world, I strongly criticize the government's drive to limit personal freedoms.

In a world where technology has become a powerful means to regulate all aspects of human life, we must also consecrate personal freedoms and raise their status on our moral scale. If we fail to defend rights and personal freedoms, even the grim ones such as suicide, then we may reach a day where we become eternal prisoners to time, powerless, waiting for its next move, no matter how cruel it may be.   – Janna Abdallah

I was finally able to get my thoughts together and finish the article a week after Jamal's passing. It was my duty to communicate his thoughts, despite the rippling chest pains bedeviling me, which made me doubt every line I had written in that article.

How could I defend "personal freedoms" which not only culminated in death, but also inflicted almost-unbearable pain upon the family members left behind? How could I defend someone's right to die, and not defend his loved ones' right to avoid the trauma they'd experience after his death? How could I defend a brother's desire to die, he leaving his sister, his lifelong friend, alone in this world, the void he left behind crushing her, what was left of him in her memories and scattered photos torturing her, things which time wouldn't erase or the days wouldn't ease?

I had blamed and reprimanded myself throughout the preceding week. How did my heart make me obey and stand by silently as I watched Jamal's eventually fatal strokes occur one after the other without interfering? Had I lost my mind when I forced myself to respect his choice? Why didn't I take him on more boldly? Why didn't I beg him more forcefully? Why didn't I intervene and ask his doctors to activate the nanobots in his body? I could have saved him. I could have held onto him. But I didn't. Did I not know the actual loss that his death represented? Or didn't I realize that this separation would be permanent?

I felt horrible. I was content to guarantee my own opportunity to give birth, letting Jamal waste away because I had a replacement. How appalling of me! I thought of his last days as a difficult time that would soon pass and be done with. Something inside me looked towards the end of his suffering. I was looking forward to the peace that would come after it. What sort of peace was I talking about? I was stupid, just as I was the day that Mom died. How crazy I was. Which loony finds peace in getting rid of those people closest to her heart?

How cruel the puzzle of fate is when we realize that the cemetery within us grows the longer we live and the more we cling on to life.

Abla also couldn't bear Jamal's death. She left me and joined him. She added her own tombstone to the cemetery inside me when I found her two days after Jamal's death on Jamal's deathbed; a lifeless corpse, curled into a ball of yearning, as if she was waiting for him to come back, hug her, and take her with him. She could have waited for me to be healed of his death, but instead she seized the opportunity to increase my pain and rub salt in my wounds.

I left my article and immersed myself in the numerous certificates that Jamal had been awarded during his career. A certificate of appreciation from the global stem-cell conference at Biocant in Portugal in 2021 for his development of a new technology that implanted stem cells into the brain and eliminated Parkinson's. A prize awarded to him by the American Methylocella Foundation (which was working to lengthen human life) for his invention of an effective way to double the lifespan of a lab rat, an amazing feat at that time. A certificate, awarded by the global conference for regenerative medicine that was held in Leipzig, Germany in 2025, to recognize Jamal's contributions to the development of the Alzheimer's vaccine. Tons of medical achievements guaranteeing Jamal's name would be up there with the greatest human beings in modern history.

How great you were, Jamal: you saved the world, but you didn't save yourself!

His funeral was a colossal affair. High-ranking state functionaries attended, headed by King Hussein II and Prime Minister Thoraya Mahmoud. Scientists from Jordan and the world over gathered in the garden of our house, praying for him and praising his achievements. We, his family, gathered to comfort one another, supporting each other through this ordeal.

Death today was harsher than it was in the past because it had become rare. I left Jihan and Khalid to manage the funeral. I wasn't able to take it on at a time when I found it difficult to simply get out of bed. Zaid didn't leave my side for a minute. He was tremendously compassionate, something I had missed in him for a while. Kameel would drop by daily to console me as well. Just seeing him put me at ease. I attributed it to my conviction that his presence meant Mom was nearby.

CHAPTER 15

OMAR, THE YOUNG MAN

O MAR appeared on stage. He bounded in energetically, carrying a large 3D spoon on his back. His captivating smile dominated his facial features – he seemed confident, proud, like I had never seen him before. His movements were quick and his body slender with the disappearance of the small hump on his upper back. His eyes were brighter, enlarged after the flabby skin around them had disappeared and his bloated eyelids had been drained. He drew closer to Hilda the host, who greeted him and asked, "Omar, how are you feeling today?"

He responded by giving her the thumbs up in front of the crowd as a sign that he felt better than ever, and afterwards he confirmed this by pumping the great spoon on his back up and down above his shoulders ten times before putting it to one side on the floor.

"Seems Omar is planning to take part in the Olympics one day," Hilda said, laughing. She directed her next words to the audience: "In the four weeks since the beginning of the show, Omar's age has been dialed back four decades. Today

Omar is considered middle-aged going by prevailing wisdom. Our dear viewers, tonight we're giving the contestants the chance to celebrate a particular person who holds great importance in their lives." Hilda looked at Omar. "Tell us, who's the person that left such an impression on your life that you'd want to thank today?"

Omar brought the microphone to his mouth, directed his words to the camera, and said, "There's someone whose kindness I'll never forget. A beautiful woman who'd shine on me every day with the rising of the morning sun... her smile would lift me up during the hard times while her sympathy and generosity were pillars of support in times of need. She's the mother I never knew, even though her return to youth makes her come across as my granddaughter... you all know her well from her great writing, but I, even though I don't know how to make many of the letters, I'm the one who knows her humanity and kindness of heart the most. Today I'd like to thank the esteemed writer Janna Abdallah." Omar ended his speech to loud applause from the audience.

The camera panned back to focus on Hilda, who gushed, "Before we leave you viewers with the segment about Omar-and Janna's relationship, let's have a look first at the surprise that the program team has put together for him." Hilda approached Omar and said, "There's a visitor we've invited to follow today's episode with us in the studio today. You ready to receive this special guest?"

Omar nodded his head, showing his readiness while Hilda finished her words by welcoming me: "Viewers, welcome with me the acclaimed journalist Janna Abdallah."

I quickly made my way up to the stage to meet Omar, anxious to see him again now that vitality had returned to his body. The studio was exuberant, reflecting Omar's glowing, joyful face. I drew closer to him and felt a need to hug him. For the first time during all my years of knowing him, the social barrier between us crumbled.

Our communication in the past hadn't gone further than comforting one another with good wishes and a few words, bodily contact that didn't go past the meeting of our palms. Each of us was careful not to traverse the distance that each one's social class imposed. The frame of my car and box of gum in his hand used to determine the social lines of defense, even though we sometimes tried to ignore them. We sailed through a brief human dialogue allowed by the short time-spans between the changing of red and green traffic lights.

Embracing him today translated him into a friend. My touching his body and feeling his liveliness washed away my guilty feelings that had characterized my relationship with him. His pleasant smell and clean clothes put my conscience at ease. I looked at him closely and marveled at his grand transformation. Momentarily I saw Jamal's face in his and teared up.

If only Jamal had changed his opinion in his final days, he would be here today with Omar's energy, zest, and joy. I would have been able to bring him with me on stage to take part in celebrating Omar. I shook off Jamal's image from my mind and held Omar's hand. We walked towards the contestants' corner. We sat among them and watched the segment.

Omar appeared onscreen weaving between cars by the

traffic light at the entrance of Abdoun. It seemed like the opening scenes of the segment had been filmed during the first days of the show, as Omar appeared old, brittle in movement. But the picture changed after a minute, and he now bore an appearance closer to his current form, active, humming tunes from contemporary songs as he greeted drivers and wished them a great day.

After another minute, my black Land Rover appeared at the traffic light. Omar approached my car window and greeted me. The camera zoomed in on my face, my sunglasses coming into view. I picked my handbag from the empty passenger seat beside me and fished for my wallet. I took out a note and pressed it into Omar's hand, and he reciprocated with pieces of gum.

The host's voice accompanying the video said, "Dear viewers, you may believe that after many long years of routinely standing at the same traffic light, boredom defines a gum-seller's life. Well that's not the case here; our pal Omar shows us the opposite of this. Omar considers his job one of the most thrilling, when you take into account the amount of influential people that he meets every morning. Omar has the ability to read the country's mental state overall by reading the faces of people as they're on their way to work. He's like a barometer measuring air pressure. He'll find a daily trend in the general mood reflected on their faces. He gives greater weight to the faces of those who hold an important position in the civil service. On this basis he established a formula based on if it was a good or bad day, and on the days where the mood was bad, Omar cut short his work and made his way to the nearby mosque, drawing out his prayers, beseeching God to have compassion on his servants. As for the better days where the mood was jovial, he would extend his hours to be blessed by the smiles and warm faces of those passing by. Omar considers the writer Janna Abdallah a lifelong friend, and one of the most important faces that he depends on to gauge the general mood. He says that her face never lies, and so he found it easy to read what her wide eyes and sharp facial lines tried to hide. It was as if there was an unspoken agreement between them both, with Janna reading the daily newspaper before leaving for work, reflecting what she read on her face for Omar to know how he should conduct his prayers that day. He knew well that her concern for general society always took precedence over her personal issues, and that's why he depended on her more than others."

The segment continued showing photos and short video clips of Omar and me over the years. It showed a few pictures of us from my college days, with Omar looking like a kid. One of them was of us sitting on a wooden bench next to the main boulevard leading into the University of Jordan campus, next to the College of Literatures. He was talking to me about something or the other – it's impossible to remember now. Another picture of us in my car at the northern entrance of the university reminded me that I used to conspire with him sometimes and help him sneak onto campus.

It also showed a short video clip of us at the Abdoun traffic light in 2026, the year in which panic spread throughout the population after antibodies lost their ability to fight bacteria. I was wearing a surgical mask and gloves as I handed

Omar some change. He was also wearing a mask that I had bought for him at that time. In that era, I used to take pieces of gum from him and throw them out straight after, scared of contracting a disease. That year, from what I remember, Omar lost his wife and two daughters – two young girls back then – to tuberculosis. I also lost family and friends, and nearly lost my life, too.

Afterwards they also showed a short scene of me giving Omar a black bag full of clothes. I was giving away some clothes of Zaid's and mine to whoever needed them after we had stopped wearing them. At the end of the segment was a shot of Omar helping me change my car tire, and a picture of him as he stood in a crowd of men at Jamal's funeral last month.

At the end of the segment, just before a commercial break, the camera panned back to focus on Hilda, who said, "Dear viewers, stay with us. We'll be back after the break to follow the contestants as they write their wills stating how they will like their lives to be run during their new childhood until they are adults again. Once their memories are wiped clean, they'll be fresh slates, and will need to prepare for the future. After that, we'll announce last week's results and the ranking of the contestants."

I seized the ad break as an opportunity to have a chat with Omar. After I complimented him once more on regaining his strength, and on his brilliant performance on the show as he had captured the viewers' hearts in such a short period of time, I asked him about what he intended to record in his will.

He didn't answer me. He chuckled and said he'd leave it

a surprise. I didn't press him but I couldn't control myself. I held his gaze as I asked, "Omar, why don't you pull out of the show?"

Clearly taken aback, he asked, "Pull out from the show?"

"Pull out now, or after a week or two. Don't wait until you reach your childhood, only to lose your identity and memories."

Omar laughed at my suggestion. As he was talking to me, he was preoccupied with surveying the preparation on stage for the next segment, and the adoring audience. He responded, "It's no good to pull out, 'cause they put a steep penalty clause in our contracts if we do that." He got up as if he had remembered something urgent. "I've gotta go to the bathroom. I'll be back in a jiffy."

Before he disappeared behind the stage décor, he looked at me and said, "After all Janna, I want to forget. My life's been tough. I want to erase all of it and start over... a blank page." He bent over to kiss my forehead and left me to cry by myself after that.

Why did everyone want to leave me and start over?

CHAPTER 16

A PROPER GOODBYE

SINCE Jamal's death, I came to feeling a closeness to Zaid that I'd been missing for years. He came across as tender, reminding me of how he had stood by my side at the passing of each of my parents. He would treat me with utter gentleness, holding my palms and kissing them whenever the opportunity presented itself. He would stretch out his palm and deftly shift a lock of my hair from the front of my face behind my ear, and plant a kiss on my forehead when I was in thrall of past illusions. He would pull me to his chest and wrap me in a bear hug whenever I collapsed and cried in the face of my new reality.

If you lose someone close to you, you appreciate the importance of those who are left behind, or maybe it's a way of consoling oneself to grab onto those of our loved ones who remain. This truth was of mutual relevance to us. It was as if, like me, he felt the sharpness of the separation and realized its shocking implications. The pain of losing Jamal purified our relationship and sucked out the repellent force that had been bouncing between us. Or was it the strange mutual understanding that between us was a shared duty to respect and feel affection for the other's desire – his dream to return to childhood, mine to bring back my mother? Our shared understanding confirmed to us that our connection by marriage was immune to time.

We both knew very well that his next adventure could be considered a type of parting, a separation, but we didn't veer from our agreement on it. I believe that there's a weakness inside of me, a weakness that made me surrender to Jamal's desire to die, and which left me helpless in front of Zaid's desire to depart as well. Or maybe we realized at this stage of our lives that our relationship needed this type of break to survive, a seasonal trimming of its dead branches so that the stalk could return, growing back much stronger.

But I couldn't share in his adventure with this sort of relationship between us, without a proper goodbye to confirm each one's commitment to the other, without him helping me through his budding childhood years until he reached adulthood again and returned to reclaim his previous role as a husband in my life.

The night before we went for the medical consultation to prepare Zaid for this new journey, he was standing in the corner of the kitchen holding a knife, smearing some chocolate spread on a slice of bread. I was perched on the couch in the living room, scrutinizing him, watching his every move. We were in our almost-matching pajamas – blue pants with white stripes and white tops.

"Zaid, make me a sandwich like yours," I asked sweetly.

"Sure thing," he crooned back. He carried the sandwich

he had finished preparing back to me. "Here you go m'lady." He went back to the kitchen, picked up another slice of bread and started preparing another sandwich.

I put my sandwich to the side, and took a deep breath. I hesitated a bit, shy about what I was about to do, but in no time I stood up and made my way towards him. I approached him soundlessly and wrapped my arms around his waist from behind. I kissed his upper back, whispering, "Thanks for the sandwich."

He turned towards me, hugged me tightly, and stroked my back with his upper arm. He kissed me between my eyes and afterwards stepped back a bit, careful not to smear me with his chocolate-covered fingers. I took his index finger and licked off the chocolate, giggling like a schoolgirl. He looked at me. He smiled. He fell silent, tense, and moved his head as he searched for a napkin to wipe his hand on. He cleaned his fingers and came back to hugging me. I laid my head on his chest and listened to his breath. A few seconds later he whispered in my ear, "I have to go to the bathroom."

He left me confused, embarrassed by what I'd done. Was I wrong to think that I, without speaking, would be able to revive our sexual relationship? Was I deluded in trying to bring it back in this way after a three-year hiatus, without any verbal communication or spoken mutual understanding about renewing it?

Had my body language been clear to Zaid only for him to refuse it because it had caught him off guard? Or had he run away because he didn't want me? Maybe I hadn't been clear enough, so he left confused, finding an excuse to run off to the bathroom? I felt pretty humiliated. Here he was rejecting me and ignoring me after I pressured myself to dare to save our relationship.

I picked myself up and went to our room. I grabbed a magazine and began to flip through it. When he returned, I ignored him. He looked at me and asked, "You didn't eat your sandwich?"

"I'm not hungry anymore," I answered, avoiding his gaze. He drew closer.

Standing at a distance from the bed, he asked, "Janna, is something wrong?"

"No, nothing's wrong."

He stood for a moment and stared intently at me as I read the magazine, after which he got into bed next to me and picked up his own book to read. Some minutes passed by, with each of us seemingly lost in reading. But I actually was being pummeled by waves of anger. I couldn't control myself any longer. I set the magazine to one side and irritably said Zaid's name. He looked at me wordlessly, waiting for me to go on. I asked, "Why'd you do that?"

I expected him to pretend he had no idea what I was talking about, but he didn't. He answered quietly, "I'm sorry, Janna, about the way it happened… I wasn't expecting that."

Even though his excuse infuriated me, I quickly apologized: "I'm sorry if I went about this the wrong way, I was thinking maybe we could just try. I want to feel that everything is fine between us before you become a kid again. It'll be hard for me to wait for you until you're an adult again to be my husband, and for our relationship to return to an intimate one. I wanted to wish you farewell."

"Farewell? I'm not going anywhere, I'll still be with you."

"I know, but I meant saying goodbye to you as my husband. Because it'll be weird between us when you become a kid."

"I'll be a kid, but I'll still be your husband. Nothing's going to change."

"Zaid, how will nothing change? Yes, you'll still be my husband, but only on paper as the nature of our relationship will change until you grow up again. It won't be easy for you or me. It'll be a strange setup, and I'm sure there won't be any romance or sex going on between us."

He fell silent for the first time, thinking of the ramifications of his upcoming adventure, and afterwards suggested, "You want us to try, Janna?"

"Do *you* want to try?"

"Now?"

I had in fact lost my desire after he turned me down, especially as I had made an effort to rekindle the desire within me over the past few days. But due to the sensitivity of the situation, I masked my feelings behind the need to break this sexual barrier between us. It would be a bad idea to show my hesitation if I wanted to convince him that I wanted him. So I responded confidently, smiling, "Now!", even though I was utterly terrified that this attempt would fail and confirm that we were no long able to enjoy each other physically.

He straightened up in bed and stretched out his hand, beckoning for me to draw closer. I pulled the duvet from him and straddled his thighs. I held his head and started kissing it. Slow kisses that would help get me going – and him too. I moved away from his lips a little and kissed his forehead, I smiled, happy to be feeling what I feared I wouldn't feel. I went back to kissing his mouth and felt his arousal surge to a crescendo within him as he pulled the tumescent member from between my hands, turned me on my back, and spread his body across mine.

Zaid wasn't a big man, only a few centimeters taller than me, and I was considered short. His body was more on the slender side, and even though I wished he were taller, I had gotten used to his frame. I liked those fine, slender biceps as well as the blond fuzz that covered his chest and stomach.

It was as if the hiatus between our last sexual liaison and now had been enough to erase my knowledge of his body. Even though he was in front of me every day, morning and night, I felt I was learning his body anew. Maybe this hiatus is what refreshed our nocturnal encounter and brought back some zing to our relationship. I clung to him and laid my head on his shoulder after we had finished, contented with my decision to hang onto my husband and make our bond last.

I left him after savoring the afterglow and went to the bathroom to take a shower. He followed me and we showered together like two newlyweds. I felt something new growing within me. When we returned to bed, my craving for a Nutella sandwich came back. I got up and brought it in from the sitting room, and devoured it with satisfaction.

When I turned off the light and put my head on the pillow, Kameel's image returned to keep me company. But his presence wasn't as strongly felt as it had been previously. I think that my yearning for him had disappeared with Jamal's departure, or maybe it hadn't disappeared but I had just wrapped it under the rubble of being separated from Jamal, and my realization of how much I needed Zaid in my life.

I closed my eyes wishing that the way I felt right then would stay the same, unchanged.

But it didn't.

CHAPTER 17

DEATHBED

L IFE lives on the edge of death just as death is found at life's end. Until the time of the Black Death, doctors in Europe had no urge to develop the practice of medicine. The Black Death not only stole away hundreds of millions of human lives during the Middle Ages but also engendered methodical approaches to saving lives, as the plague forced mankind to become aware of the need to invent new procedures to preserve general health and manage medical facilities. The plethora of tragic deaths during that dark episode spurred mankind to focus on clinical medicine based on the exacting study of physiology instead of analyses steeped in astrology and superstitions.

In the first third of this century, the cycle repeated itself once mankind woke up to the ineffectiveness of one of their most important weapons in resisting pernicious antigens – antibodies – and death returned to reign over the world. It was a rude awakening for the human race and an earth-shattering shock to the medical corps. When it came to our comprehension of the universe, we seemed to be at the peak of our information renaissance, only to realize at that juncture that we still didn't know a lot about of the pillar of our existence: the human body.

Biochemistry's inability to match the rapid evolutionary development of microscopic beings called for the interventional help of biotechnology. And even though it was relatively new science without much vested interest at first, the fear of death refocused the efforts of this science on speeding up the growth of this sector, transforming it over just a few years into a gigantic industry that played a key role in wiping out a number of human illnesses – first off the list, old age.

Till now, we still don't know all the minutiae of the bioprocesses in the human body, but the scientific advancements of nanotechnology have supplied our bodies with an intelligent line of defense that has bolstered our immune system, refreshed life, and toughened it against death in a way that wasn't possible before.

In my first go at youth, I was a first-rate adventurer, reckless, hasty, a believer in the philosophy that if you don't live on the edge of death, you won't feel that you're actually living. I lived recklessly and considered it life on the edge. I now consider those moments as death on the edge of life. Maybe my morbid nature was an escape from Mom's disease, from the death that she planted in my heart before she departed. I was chasing risks with no awareness of the fallout, in the same way insects at night chase after a source of light. I didn't realize this until the moment I almost fell from the edge of the world straight into death's embrace.

Just as Jamal saw Mom and Dad come to welcome him

at his departure, I also saw Mom when I was in the hospital bed one night.

My mom entered my hospital room surrounded by a field of flowers. She approached my bed slowly, even though I was burning up with a longing to touch her. She didn't take me with her, she didn't speak to me that night, but walked round my bed scattering white daffodils as if they were a shroud. After she finished, she threw me a garland of flowers. I remember how we used to make them when I was a kid. She whispered, "Put it round your neck and get up darling. Nothing's wrong with you."

She disappeared in the blink of an eye while my coughing intensified. Strong relentless coughs that I felt tearing my chest apart as they filled my mouth with sticky sputum. I stretched out my weak hand, my body trembling, to get a tissue from the box beside the bed to spit out the gooey mess in my mouth. The tissue became soiled with a red color I dreaded seeing.

At that moment I was certain that I had a date with death despite Mom's words in my dream, as I had gotten accustomed to seeing her and speaking to her in those days of my sickness, whenever my temperature jumped over forty degrees.

I was one of tens of thousands who fell victim to tuberculosis. One of a flood of humans who fell ill when existing tuberculosis treatments had lost their effectiveness. One of millions who stood bewildered at the staggering inability of medicine – a discipline that we believed had reached its peak.

As a journalist, I had documented a number of tragedies at this stage of the epidemic; I realized the magnitude of the disaster more than others. I knew the stages of death one by one. I knew how a patient's face would look like before being infected, how fatigue would overcome him, and how after a few days, persistently worse coughs would afflict him and raise his temperature. After that came trembling, feebleness, and gradual loss of weight until he became a bag of bones before breathing his last.

I observed the anguish of different patients' psyches: that desperate, defeated woman; that terrified hysterical lady; and the one who pretended to be healthy and still clung to hope of a cure. The tuberculosis bacterium doesn't discriminate or differentiate; to the contrary of the news reports that were focusing on the importance of one's state of mind to be cured, death would reap a bounteous harvest with harsh randomness. It saw no difference between patients, instead it left behind faces as it met them... whether they were frowning, hopeful, or fighting to go out with a smile their family would remember after they had gone.

The case that affected me the most was of a young girl, seven years old, that I met in Al-Koura district in the north of the Kingdom, the epicenter of the epidemic where only a few people survived to remember the darkness of that time. Zaid warned me against going, and tried as much as he could to stop me. But I was, like I said, reckless. I had established my own newspaper a year before and worked doggedly to transform journalism in Jordan with unprecedented professionalism. In my opinion, the medical calamity was an irreplaceable opportunity to advance our work and establish our existence. For the sake of sharing my philosophy with the management of my foundation, and to succeed in leading the investigators who worked with me – a team that didn't exceed a dozen – I had to go out into the real world and inspire them. So I didn't listen to Zaid or heed any of the warnings about going into the areas that were heartlands of the outbreaks, at a time when governments believed the best way to work with such areas was to quarantine them from the world.

I noticed her standing on her doorstep, her hair brown, curly, and sticking out in all directions, hanging down over her honey-colored eyes. Her eyes were tired and sad, an antithesis of the spark of life that accompanied children of her age. Her clothes were ragged, not suitable for the cold of the Kingdom's frigid winters. Her feet were exposed in flip-flops, at whose tips plastic Minnie Mouse heads bobbled. In her hand was a doll with a laughing face. She called out to me, "Miss… Miss!" I approached her with my photographer flanking me.

"Mama's really thirsty."

"Where's Mama, honey?" I asked her.

"Inside. In bed. Sick." She coughed. She hugged her doll to her chest like she was getting ready to sleep. She coughed again before adding, "Baba was thirsty. He died." She coughed twice more. "Hani was thirsty." Coughing again, she continued: "He died. Suha was thirsty. She died." More coughing. "Mama", she coughed several times more sharply before rasping, "thirsty…"

She was silent for a bit and then raised and showed me her cloth doll, which was dripping water. She croaked, "I give her something to drink all the time so she doesn't get thirsty."

I hesitated before getting any closer. I pulled up my medical gloves to ensure that they covered the greatest amount of arm skin possible and pulled the mask firmly over my mouth. I took the doll from her hand and said, "She's really cute, what's her name?"

"Maya."

"And you, what's your name?"

"Maya."

The dusty wind was turbulent enough to lodge grains of sand in my eyes. I closed them hoping to resist my need to rub them. I hugged the girl with my arm and pulled her into my waist. I felt a longing to kiss her head; maybe it was indicative of my yearning to protect her from what she'd gone through. I grabbed her hand and pulled her towards the house. I patted her head, saying, "Let's get going then. Let's go in and give Mama some water to drink."

I entered the house warily. It was cold and dark. We took a few steps in the hallway towards the sitting room. The house seemed deserted. It was furnished with old, scattered furniture, with cracked broken glass all around. Or it wasn't abandoned but lived in by a family that didn't possess what it took to establish their presence inside the house.

I heard the sound of coughing from inside and watched Maya as she opened the hallway door leading to the bedroom. I followed her in with the photographer behind me, coughing as I choked on the rotting stench that emanated from the place.

In the bedroom, Maya's mother lay in agony on the bed. She was the picture of a living mummy, her eyes hollowed with her facial bones protruding, her small frame trembling under the blanket. She was unable to sense our presence because of her battle with an aggressive fever. But she regained a bit of consciousness when Maya drew near to her. Maya jumped onto the bed next to her and shook her shoulders several times while calling, "Mama, Mama, Mama, you wanna drink something?"

Her mother stretched out her quivering hand to push Maya away, as if her presence with her in bed annoyed her. She looked at me with empty eyes and said to Maya, "Here, your aunt has come. Go with her darling and I'll catch up with you later." A violent fit of coughing took over, and she spewed out squirts of blood-laced phlegm.

I approached her, unsure how to help, and introduced myself, "I'm Janna Abdallah, a journalist. With me is my photographer Rashid Ahmed," I gestured to Rashid, then went on. "Your situation is critical, Mama Maya, we have to take you to the hospital."

Her eyes protruded as if I had threatened her with something terrifying. Her trembling intensified in bed and she started pleading with me, "No hospital, no, no." She looked at the wall beside me, her voice rising, growing stronger as she addressed her absent husband, deluded. "Abu Hani, they want to take me to the hospital!" She raised a threatening finger at him and ordered, "Get up and get rid of them. I won't leave the kids here." Her mind drifted for a moment. She then shifted her gaze in another direction and said irritability, "Hani, take your sister and go play in your room." She fell silent after the apparitions of her children went off to the next room. She stifled her cough and instructed me, "Take Hania with you to the hospital, and treat her, take care of her." She wagged her finger at me as she went on, "She's in your hands now. Got it? You take care of her till Judgment Day." She coughed, sorrow writ large on her face, before tearfully adding, "I'll stay here with the kids."

Her state of weakness took me back to the last days of Mom's life. Once again I was unable to help, as my eyes followed a child that had lost her family. I stood paralyzed as I watched a mother push her away, forced to as a part of her final preparations before her death.

I saw myself in Hania, or Maya as she called herself. I saw the agony of separation from my mother that I had suffered taking shape in the future of this child when she would become aware of what was happening this very moment.

At that time I was ready to do anything to protect her, to spare her those difficult feelings of loneliness, loss, and disorientation. I got close to the bed and scooped Maya up in my arms. I hugged her like I'd never hugged anyone before. I whispered in her ear soothing words that I don't remember now. I was ready to carry her with me to Amman, to treat her, adopt her, and compensate her for the motherly tenderness she had lost. But it seemed that she didn't want that for her future. Destiny had written a different plan other than what I wished for her, pulling her from this world a week later to have her join her mother, leaving me behind bedridden, lost, frailer than ever. I don't know if destiny also had plans for my end at the time or if it was a twist planted in my life path so that I would move on with a greater awareness and appreciation of life. A humbling that made me hang onto this world in a way that I had done before.

Maya left but she planted a seed within me, reviving feelings of motherhood that I had been ignoring. A want that had grown over the years in spite of my resistance. I fought it until I lost my ability to give birth. I buried it among the hopes and wishes that I had failed to achieve in my life.

But destiny brought this desire back to life today. It gave me a new life. It held out to me everything I needed to achieve an old dream and start a new phase I had high hopes for.

And just as my stubborn craving for life increased after I smelled the stench of death, my desire to create a new life increased when fumes of death covered my world and wrenched Jamal from my arms.

CHAPTER 18

I'LL SPLIT MY GOD-GIVEN FORTUNE WITH HER

I GOT used to Jihan being one of the biggest obstacles standing between me and my dreams. Like tiny shards of rock, she embedded herself in the roof of my throat, blocking any food, air, everything else that refreshes me in this world. It was as if all the gifts that fate had for me were signed in both our names. Contrary to the norm of humanity, where even identical twins were born with blessings allocated to each one personally, my own blessings had to be divided with Hell-lady. We each eventually agreed to be content with our portion, or we'd end up fighting over it when we couldn't agree on how best to divvy it up.

With Jihan, money was rarely the issue; what annoyed me was having to compete with her for the attention of the people in both of our lives. I mean, I was used to competing with her in journalism, her jostling for every big and small thing, including the narrow space that my daily column occupied. Even though I blamed Jamal for claiming two-thirds of the inheritance when my father died, when the will had actually divided it equally between the two of us, my blame was short-lived. I caught myself and resolved the issues between us after a short time, afraid that Jihan would whisk him completely out of my life.

If it were up to her, Jihan would close off the inheritance to me completely. In order to avoid her wrath, Jamal took the middle ground between us and claimed to be applying Sharia law, even though he knew that doing so meant I would get less than half of Dad's assets, with Jamal taking twice as much. But I now know that doing this to me in order to please his wife weighed heavily on his conscience and tormented him for the rest of his life.

He didn't ponder on his guilt except in the moment where he grabbed the pen and signed away to me his right to life. He looked over at me, satisfied. He kissed my hands like I used to kiss his. He took my hands and placed them on my stomach gently, and with a smile congratulated me.

I remember how nasty Jihan was after my dad died. As if it had been her own father's inheritance and not my father's. She became unhinged and kept on repeating, "Sharia law is clear, Janna: men inherit twice the amount of assets as women." As if she were the guardian of Sharia law or the scion of our lady Fatimah, Muhammad's daughter herself! She invoked Sharia even though she didn't know a thing about it. She stuck as much as possible to trying to get my share after failing to convince me of relinquishing the inheritance completely. She would add coolly, "Honestly, what would you want with the inheritance? You still have your husband! He's doing well; he has money. Your brother hasn't even finished his studies."

Despite all this – the money that she took from my family's wealth, first after my father's passing and then after Jamal's passing – nothing tormented me as much as those years where I saw her domineer Jamal and control the extent of my relationship with him. She considered herself to be in a race with me, or in an animal struggle to mark our territory. I fully appreciated her pride at what she had achieved in controlling him, especially as she reiterated this at every opportunity she got.

She would usually reinforce her dominance by minimizing my involvement in Jamal's private affairs, to prove to me that there was no way of having a relationship with him except through her. I'll never forget that dark day when I was speaking with a group of my friends on the university campus. I felt two cold hands slither around my head and cover my eyes, and I heard Jihan's voice: "Guess who?" I knew right away, more from her overpowering perfume than from her voice. I pushed her fingers away, irritated, saying, "Jihan, what are you doing? You hurt me!"

She quipped back, "Sorry, I didn't mean to." She stretched out her hand and patted me on the shoulder as if to wipe away all the pain she had caused. She grabbed her mobile excitedly, shoved it in front of my face, and said, "Janna, look!"

I glanced and saw a photo of a beautiful diamond ring, but I didn't catch her drift. I said cautiously, "Very nice."

She pulled the phone back from me and said, "We saw it yesterday. I really liked it! I was thinking, *khalas*, I'll just buy it."

"You and Jamal?" I asked, disapproving.

"Yes, me and Jamal. I mean, who else would I have gone with?" She added, "Jamal proposed."

I felt as if I had been slapped across the face. How could Jamal take this step without consulting me? "Oh really? Jamal proposed?" My reaction wasn't the most diplomatic, but I didn't care. I couldn't bring myself to congratulate her; instead, I dared to openly protest, "Jihan, you're both still young. What's the rush?"

"It's not about us being rushed. We've been engaged for a year or two just so that we could see each other and go out comfortably," she answered, full of confidence.

Everything was planned and set out for him by Jihan. She knew her bullseyes and knew how to hit them. Nothing was in my hands. I dashed away from her and called Jamal. I was furious and spoke to him resolutely without indulging in any chitchat.

"Jamal, you proposed to Jihan?"

He softly responded, "Yes, last night we talked about it over dinner."

"Is it normal for you to decide such things on your own?" I rebuked.

"Yes it is. What's the problem?" he answered, his tone sharpening.

"*What's the problem*? No problem at all, in fact. In any case, congrats." A lump settled in my throat as I wished him well. His stubbornness was always greater than mine. His desire to pull away and distance himself paralyzed me. Just as death would later steal him away right in front of me, Jihan ripped him away from me as well. He had chosen her, fully aware, his mental acuity unimpeachable just as it would be when he chose his end and ran away from me.

But Jihan was more merciful towards me than death. Even though she had changed him after he met her, she didn't completely cut him out of my life. Not because she didn't wish to, but because she didn't succeed in doing so. She tried several times to put a monkey wrench in the works but almost always failed because our consanguineous bond was a Trojan horse that always kept us connected in the midst of her machinations, something I relied on to reclaim a part of my brother.

She succeeded once. It was when I fell prey to tuberculosis and didn't find him beside me. Jihan forbade him from visiting me, scared that I would infect him or others in her family. She alienated him from me when I was at my weakest and at a time when I was in need of those dearest to me. I needed Jamal to help choose life over death, but he withdrew from me and left me whispering, praying in silence.

I would have given in to death if it hadn't been for Zaid's love and the appearance of Mom's ghost urging, "Get up, honey, nothing's wrong with you."

She was like sunshine or a warm cup of morning coffee. I heard her repeat, "Get up, honey, nothing's wrong with you." My soul smiled and my face lit up. Her words became an invitation for me to enter into a new day in spite of my mental or physical condition at that time.

In that time of sickness, I promised myself not to let Jamal's name pass my lips or to call him my brother. I gave up on him completely and left him to Jihan. I stopped taking his calls and didn't open the front door of my house when he remorsefully knocked on it after my recovery. Exhausted, I would stand in my nightshirt behind the door watching him through the peephole as he stood on the other side, waiting, tense. He would move to the right and then to the left before pressing the doorbell again or knocking on the door. I gathered up my strength and restrained myself from opening the door for him, even though every ring of the doorbell shook my core and every knock shredded my inner being.

The first time he came was after I had been out of the hospital for a week. The next day, he came back at the same time and stood in the same place. And after that, he came again after two days, and then after a week, then a month until he lost hope of making up with me.

I didn't forgive him until years later, after I realized that the hurt of my anger towards him was pulling me down instead of him. It grew within me and spread, hiding from me any glimmer of happiness. It pressed on my nerves and pained me the more time passed.

How ironic fate is: all this took place at Jihan's hands at a time when she wanted to take advantage of my media influence to promote a new drug that Jamal had developed which restored flexibility to old, tight blood vessels.

She called me to tell me that Jamal missed me terribly, and to relay the depth of his sadness at being distanced from me. What she said to me next got through my defenses: "Janna, you've only got one brother, and he doesn't have anyone but you. You only have each other." She then confessed that she had kept him from me.

She brought him to visit me at home after she had extracted from me a promise not to turn him away. I longed to meet him after four years of us being cut off from one another. And when he arrived, my door was open to him, my arms open to embrace him once more into my life. Jihan came in front of him, carrying a box that contained a cake. He followed her slowly and waited for her to finish greeting and kissing me. When it came his turn to greet me, he stretched out his hand to shake mine shyly, but I ignored it. I looked at his face silently before I moved in and hugged him. I really squeezed him hard as I tried in vain to hold back the stream of tears pouring down onto his shoulder. I wiped them away and invited him inside as if nothing had happened.

How transparent Jihan was, there to carry out her mission during our reunion. As soon as I had brought a cup of coffee, she shifted her position and asked, "Did you hear about the new medicine that Jamal came up with?"

I nodded my head and congratulated him on his achievement.

"It's going to cause a medical revolution. Strokes the world over will disappear and high blood pressure will become a thing of the past. We want you to orchestrate a PR campaign to announce its discovery."

"Sure, I can do some good publicity," I responded, staring at Jamal, trying to read the signs of time that had crept onto his face over the years that I hadn't been allowed to see him. I felt the betrayal of fate that had stolen from me the opportunity to watch his hairline recede and the spreading of white among the hairs that remained. I got lost in pondering the new lines that slept under his eyes, dividing his face into sections.

He was a stranger to me, far from me, cold to the point that I thought it was likely his presence here was only for Jihan, and what she had just said.

How cunning she was back then! Just like the day she had lured Jamal to marry her: she told him that she had another suitor, that she was under pressure from her mother, and that she'd be unable to turn this groom down. She pressurized him to get married to her quickly, he being afraid of losing her. Even though there was opposition from our family, his insistence left us no choice but to give in to his wishes. But at that moment, I felt that she had succeeded in imparting her wiliness to him, even though I knew that it would be impossible for her to transform him into a carbon copy of herself.

She surrendered him to me only after the signs of age had accumulated in him, and his presence became tiring instead of beneficial. That tiredness that I felt after taking care of him, that I longed for today whenever Jamal's absence tormented me. But just as a shepherd milks his goat to the last drop, Jihan didn't give up what she thought was rightfully hers.

She surprised me the day of his funeral, asking about his signature on the will stating who would inherit his right for life. I was scurrying down the hallway of the funeral hall towards the kitchen to help offer lunch to the female mourners when she blocked my path. Two plates full of *mansaf* nearly fell from my left hand, and a canister of *laban* in my right jiggled as I attempted to avoid crashing into her.

"Janna, did Jamal sign the will?" she asked.

I responded, "Yes he signed it."

I carefully raised the two plates of rice and meat, pierced the small space that she had left between herself and the wall, and walked past her. When I came back, she was waiting for me. I tried to ignore her.

She asked, "Where is it?"

"What?"

"The will."

"In the house, Jihan. Now's not the time." I left her and entered the kitchen again to put away the dirty plates that I had collected from some mourners. She followed me to the kitchen and said, "Maybe tomorrow you can bring it with you? I want to take it to the lawyer."

"Sure," I said in a bid to get rid of her. I fell silent as I watched her turn her back and leave the kitchen. As soon as she had taken her first step, I blurted, "Actually Jihan, he assigned the right to me."

CHAPTER 19

A Great Transformation

A MONTH earlier, an egg was extracted from my womb, its genetic code sucked out and replaced with the genetic code that was found in some of my mother's cells that had clung onto clothes she had left behind. The egg was then cultured to produce cell tissue, which would return to my womb and grow naturally into a complete human being after nine months.

My heart was pounding with the ferocity of church bells clanging whenever I envisioned myself linked to my mother once more with same secret thread that had brought us together a century ago. At that time, Mom would have been feeling the same mixed emotions that were drowning me today, the fear and desire to bring a new soul into this world. She was happy with her small family, grateful for her growing love for Jamal; he was her world. She was at ease with Dad being her pillar and ready to complete the square of this family by including a girl that would help her firstborn son and be a support for him in the future.

With her family around her, her concept of heaven was on

the verge of being complete, even if only for a few years. Time eventually snatched this away from her as she grew older and sicker. As for me, I was at the cusp of retrieving a piece of my heaven in an age where life could not be snatched away, and time could not be stolen. A heaven that I didn't remember much of except that she was in there, and that it wasn't complete without her.

My heart grew weak and cool sweat dripped from my forehead onto my face whenever doubts seized me and the fear of bringing a new creature into this world chained me down. The looming fear of shouldering responsibility, one that seemed more considerable than what my mind had imagined.

A new girl that would have Mom's features and not remember a thing of her past. She would grow and become aware of her consciousness and see herself as the center of the world, but at the same time cognizant of her limits, that she too would die one day, in a cold, wide world that had no consciousness, no center, and no limits. Like me, knowledge of her ability to live forever would torment her as much as the idea of being dead forever. I would be bringing her into a world where approaching the final destination had been banished, even though I knew that the lack of clarity concerning this end scared me as much as feeling it and waiting for it did.

But I got up that day bravely, like any other day, and waited for Kameel to transport me to the clinic. He was like an intermediary between my mother and me; I felt his presence was most appropriate at that moment. I wanted him close to me when my first meeting with my daughter took place, and that's why I asked the doctor to allow him inside the operating room. When I felt my consciousness slipping away due to the drugs coursing through my veins, I held his hand and squeezed it. I could almost swear that I saw his face morph into Mom's and felt her patting my head and kissing my forehead.

When I regained consciousness several hours later, I realized that a cloned soul from my mother had started growing inside me; I felt my heart constrict and a yearning for Zaid. I sobbed. Feelings of strangeness filled me when I opened my eyes and found Kameel sitting on a chair next to my bed. My topsy-turvy feelings towards him jolted me in that moment from wanting him to be there before the surgery to anxiety and uneasiness of having him beside me post-operation. A titanic transformation had shaken up my world. I frantically tried to grab onto anything that that would confirm I was still the same person and that my world was just as it had been.

I mumbled, "Kameel?"

He put the digital newspaper in his hands to one side and stood beaming beside my bed, "Thank God you're back."

"May God keep you safe too." I thanked him and asked him "What's the time?"

"Around three."

"Where's Zaid? He's late."

"We spoke earlier. I told him that you hadn't woken up yet. He was on the way. He should be here any minute," he tried to reassure me.

Last night popped into my head. Closing my eyes, I tried to forget what had happened. I took a deep breath and said faintly, not wanting anyone else to hear, "Kameel, I think

Zaid's hurt by our relationship."

"Why are you saying that? Did something happen?"

"Yesterday, after you left and I went inside the bedroom… I thought he was asleep but he was still up watching a show on TV. He ignored me. I asked him what was wrong. He didn't answer. I sensed he was upset with me." I felt thirsty and asked Kameel for a glass of water, then continued, "I've had strange feelings towards him. Ever since he started growing younger, my maternal feelings for him have grown dramatically."

Kameel pulled his chair closer and put it next to my bed and sat down. He then asked, "Okay, did he say something?"

"At first he didn't want to talk, but then he started weeping. When I pushed him to talk, he said that he felt that I was detaching myself from him."

"What did you say?"

"Nothing. I hugged him. I reassured him that he's my life and that I would never leave him or push him away… at least until he grows back up into the adult he used to be."

"You think he saw us?"

I felt embarrassed at Kameel's question, since I had been trying to skirt around what had passed between us the previous day. "I don't think so… I don't know," I answered him, trying to avoid talking about *that*. "He's had a tumultuous period, from the time that his body started shrinking. I think this whole process has been hard for him. I've felt him going back to living like a preteen. The eruption of hormones in his body makes him behave irrationally."

"Wow, his body is shrinking that fast? It's only been two weeks since he started the treatment, right?"

"He hasn't really shrunk altogether, but I just sense the change in his body and I think he feels it too and is scared of it." Kameel stretched out his hand and placed it gently on my arm, trying to reassure me that he'd be by my side during this tough time, but I felt uneasy with his bodily contact, uneasy that Zaid could come in at any moment. I pulled my arm back and said hesitantly, "Kameel, I'm embarrassed, especially as I called you to be here with me today. It's just that Zaid will be here soon and I'm worried he won't be okay with you being here."

He drew back his hovering hand, as if he'd done something wrong or forced himself on me. "I'm sorry, Janna, you're right. I'll go now."

"No, no, don't apologize, I'm the one who's sorry. Truly, thank you for coming. I couldn't have gone through with the operation without you." I couldn't believe what I was saying! He looked at me tenderly and planted a kiss on my forehead. He shifted his position and said, "Just say the word if you need anything," then left.

My eyes trailed his exit as I remembered last night.

We had left together after wrapping up at work to drink a coffee in one of the quiet Luweibdeh cafés nearby. Kameel was interning at the office for about a month, after I had put in a good word for him following our surprise encounter on the metro. That day I felt agitated, as if I really needed to talk to someone. I thought of speaking to Zaid, but I backed out of that because I realized that his thinking was no longer rational as it once was – he'd become irritable, unable to control his reactions.

Kameel sat in front of me with his usual serene demeanor, ready to listen to me obsessing. I spoke to him at great length about my simultaneous fear of motherhood and my need for it. I went over with him the insanity of the idea of getting pregnant with my mom's genetic code instead of carrying a natural pregnancy with Zaid. I justified myself, saying, "Maybe it'll be easier if I convince myself that I'm bringing someone back to life rather than creating a whole new being."

He smiled gently and responded, "If that puts you at ease, why not? I don't have a moral stance on the topic, and as long as you have the right to give birth then you're free to use it as you please. There's no right or wrong here. Maybe the only right thing is your need to do this... and the picture that you've drawn in your mind of the child who will become your mother. People will probably start judging you now, but I won't. As long as it's legal, you don't need to answer to anyone."

He could shock me sometimes with his sagacity even though he hadn't lived a quarter of the life that I had. Maybe it was because he had been born at a time when the equations of life were undergoing rapid change, and aging was becoming a choice, which protected him from the cultural bias I had developed during the years before old age was exterminated. His thoughts on "the right to pregnancy and birth" brought back to me the look on Jihan's face when I told her that Jamal had given his right to life to me.

I jumped at the chance to tell Kameel what had happened, and how I had dared to convey the good news to Jihan after she provoked me by insisting on safeguarding the will for herself on the first day of Jamal's funeral. I chuckled as I described her bulging eyes and red cheeks, occasioned by the trauma of shock, and how she subsequently surprised me with a stinging slap that made my e-lens pop out of my eye.

She had shrieked with a voice so loud that the mourners in the hall around her took notice and came to see what was happening. She shoved her finger in my face and threatened to take me to trial for my exploitation of an old, helpless man on his deathbed – her words, not mine.

The following day, I rushed to go ahead with the fertilization procedures, afraid that she would get obtain an injunction to halt the execution of the will until the matter could be decided before a court. She would have to face reality, unable to wrangle this chance from me.

What's important is that my chat with Kameel put me at ease that day, and that's why I didn't stop him from accompanying me home. Time flew by. After a cup of coffee we felt hungry and decided to move on to a nearby restaurant to have dinner. By the time I got home, it was nearly ten o'clock and the lights were off. Because of this I thought Zaid was out, and it didn't cross my mind that he could be in the bedroom. I stopped to say goodbye to Kameel when we approached the front door. I thanked him for listening to me and escorting me home.

The moon was full that night, and its radiance, along with the light of faraway streetlights and a small light bulb above the back door, pierced the garden's darkness. Kameel looked even more attractive in that moment, seemingly taller with his shadow cast on the ground behind him.

I looked into his eyes with gratitude. I drew close and kissed his cheek. I asked him if he wanted to come in to rest a bit. He responded that he had to go but asked for a glass of water.

The motion sensors inside were broken, explaining why the house didn't light up when I made my way to the kitchen. When I came back, he was standing in the living room waiting, holding a photo of Mom that I had put up with a bunch of other photos on the shelf next to the window. He quietly put the photo back in its place when I came back, took the glass from my hand, and slowly drank its contents. When he had finished he started getting ready to leave, so I took the chance to draw in close once more and thank him again.

I hugged him tightly and felt him hug me back.

I raised my head, looking at his lips, remembering an old kiss that had once stole my breath away. He was also caught in the moment. He bent his head towards me. Very gently his lips brushed my mouth.

I closed my eyes, reliving a pleasurable memory.

Just like the last time this happened, I panicked as a foreboding feeling from the second kiss, which had the same taste, sunk its magical claws into me.

I let Kameel make his way out and went into the bedroom to find Zaid perturbed, like me. I hugged him and reassured him that nothing was going to change.

CHAPTER 20

THE GATES OF HELL

A S I expected, my wrestling away of the birth-giving right from Jihan wouldn't go by unnoticed in her book. In line with her character, she had to take revenge and hurt the one who had hurt her. She tried to attack me on several fronts, from sheer anger directed at me to indefatigably discrediting me and finally punishing me in other ways for robbing her of this right.

She bared her fangs in an article she published in her news column; in it she censured me for my television appearance and what was said in the show about my relationship with Omar:

JANNA AND REALITY TELEVISION: BOURGEOISIE AT ITS WORST

Charity is a global human characteristic. Rarely do you find someone not affected by seeing another stretch out their hand to help those less fortunate, whether a handful of money or a morsel of food to the hungry or a piece of cloth to cover a homeless person. Omar bin Khattab (may Allah be pleased with him) said, "If poverty were a man, I would have killed him." But unfortunately, poverty isn't a man, and we, as a people, despite our technological progress and that of our civilization, are still unable to kill it. Our inability to get rid of poverty isn't due to a lack of natural resources or riches but rather our greedy human nature and social systems that increase the stock of the haves and treats the have-nots unjustly. Yes, we've eliminated old age and conquered illness, and our food has become even tastier with delicious dishes printed in a matter of seconds in our kitchens, but we're still unable to divide our riches in a just manner and help those of us who don't own 3D food printers or a fruit tree, or a productive animal, to curb their hunger and fill their stomachs.

A reality show like "Born Again with a Golden Spoon" provokes in me the most intense agitation at its attempt to sell itself as a noble show trying to help the poor and guarantee a new and luxurious life for those that lived a long existence of poverty and hardship – even though we know full well that the real goal of such a show is financial gain for the owners of the channels broadcasting it and for the celebrity guests. So both male and female participants, poor in every sense of the word, are only there to entertain the viewers and are victims of a capitalist innovation in further exploiting labor.

One of the episodes that most infuriated me was the one where the journalist Janna Abdallah appeared, and in particular that clip that showcased her relationship with the contestant Omar. A long-term relationship, between a well-known journalist tru-

ly born with a golden spoon in her mouth and a poor man who barely manages to curb his hunger with the meager amount that he collects on a daily basis from selling gum, was framed as being humane. According to the clip, Janna would help Omar whenever she passed by the traffic lights with an undisclosed sum, which wasn't enough for him to secure the minimum amount necessary to retrieve his youth as she had done. If she had really wanted to help him, she should have, at the very least, secured him a respectable job that would yield him a steady salary, or organize professional or technical training for him that would relieve him from his bleak situation. But she didn't do any of the above, but rather she assuaged her conscience and guilty feelings towards this poor man with a handful of change that would neither fatten him nor save him from hunger. And on top of all this, she participates in the show, confident as can be, to make herself shine and portray herself as humane, which I doubt she is. All this at Omar's expense, as she's used to doing!

Janna, for those who don't know her well – here I'm sharing some insider information – exploited her brother Jamal on his deathbed, and made him sign away his birth-giving right to her. She wickedly grabbed this rightful inheritance away from his deserving family with cunning and craftiness.

What sort of humanity do you want to sell us, Janna? And what humanity is this that the show wants to share with us?

We all know that mankind failed a long time ago since systems that don't guarantee the simplest forms of social justice took over in our societies. We are today in dire need of an urgent review of the definition of man in our current age and what characteristics are fitting for him, the most important of which we include under the banner of "humanity."

- Jihan Awad

I don't know how her editor let her publish an article that denigrated me outright, taking a stab at my credibility and reputation, even though I was her colleague at work, where it was assumed that we'd work together to embody the values of the newspaper! If I was bourgeois, exploiting the poor, then what did the newspaper that she wrote for represent? And if I was selfish, heartless, preying on the weaknesses of those closest to me for my own ends, didn't that mean that the newspaper that I worked for had similar values, and fostered them by supporting the journalists that worked for it?

I almost escalated the issue and demanded an official apology from the newspaper, but I chose to stay silent. I swallowed that blow of hers, thinking maybe it would be enough for her to vent her rage and be done with it. But it wasn't enough, as her hunger for revenge even extended to Kameel, who joined the newspaper as an intern under her wing in the local news section, which she managed.

She caught onto my interest in Kameel from the time she walked in on us during his first visit, as we chatted in the garden. She confirmed her hunch the day I brought him to the office and asked HR to find a vacancy for him, even just as an intern. She set out to close in on him from the first day he started working with us. And as usual, when she put a man in her sights, no boundaries of decency or decorum stood in her way. She would harass him openly, unconcerned by with the disapproval of work colleagues. She exaggerated her flirting with him and praised his appearance more than his writing. She drowned him in tasks whenever she saw him talking to me, and requested him to stay behind after work to finish work on trivial news pieces so that she could get closer to him. She divulged her personal affairs to him and excelled in fabricating wild stories about me.

It wasn't enough to make me look like a selfish, bourgeois woman removed from the reality of her readers; she was determined to paint me guilty and imprint that in the minds of all those around me, especially Kameel.

Her classist approach wasn't new to me. Since our first encounter in Journalism 101, she had always come across as obsessed with the bourgeoisie, Marxist thought, and critiquing capitalism. Maybe she had read and been influenced at the time by the paper that Karl Marx and Freidrich Engels published in 1848, which outlined the basic building blocks of communist thought; or maybe she hadn't read it but simply parroted and echoed those ideas without truly understanding their meanings or dimensions. She was one of those people that eagerly defended principles and theories even though the life she led stood in outright contradiction to those ideas. She attacked and lambasted what didn't concern her, because talk is easy, and creating unstudied theoretical solutions is even more so. Instead of extending a helping hand to help those poor who have been treated unjustly by the prevailing social system, even in a simple way, she would shoot an arrow up into the air that didn't change the system or help those in need.

She also contradicted herself between the lines of her article. I mean, how could she disparage the bourgeoisie and personal property when she ended her article defending her family's rights to Jamal's right to life? Shouldn't she have pushed, in the name of social justice, for the transfer of his right to life to become public instead of a private inheritance?

I'd gotten used to her jibes at me being "bougie" over time. I mean, they escaped her mouth so easily, sometimes spontaneously and at others jokingly. "Bougie Janna," she would sometimes intone, or she would lash out, "You're really a vile bougie," and cackle afterwards. I would ignore her sometimes and respond to her in like manner at others. Frankly, she was plain old jealous of me. Though I was afraid of openly declaring my ideas or confessing what went on in my mind, I knew that her words came from a place of class inferiority that she had felt ever since she got to know me and my family. I was born into a financially stable family with real estate and assets that grew over several generations, whereas she came from a family that wasn't rich and struggled to pay her college tuition.

But she, for some reason, always felt better than others, working with them with an upturned nose that didn't match her social background or level of education. Like she had achieved her future already, or maybe it was just her extreme self-confidence, which had prepared her to achieve her goal of marrying someone who would give her what she saw as her natural right: money, status, and power. She had achieved all that and more, and today owned double what I did in assets and property. Despite this, *I* was still the wicked bougie, and she was the champion of the poor, advocating for worker's rights!

In addition to her news article and getting closer to Kameel to conspire against me, she filed a lawsuit against me, accusing me of exploiting my invalid, elderly brother and stealing his right to life from her and her family. When I informed her lawyer that her case had come too late, as I was already pregnant and there was no room for judicial dispute over the right to life when a child was already growing within me, Jihan stormed into my office with her usual hysteria, threatening me, "Janna, you listen to me, and you listen good! If you don't abort what's in your womb, I promise you that you'll be forced to pay me a hefty compensation you won't be able to afford!"

She smiled devilishly and added, "And if you don't pay, and I'm sure that you won't be able to pay the amount that I'm going to demand from you, I promise you that I'll have your child put under joint trusteeship of the both of us."

I imagined my mother growing up between the both of us. She would sleep one night at mine and one night at Jihan's. Jihan would fight me for my child just as she did with Jamal. Jihan would steal my child right out of my hands like she had stolen Jamal from me.

The gravity of her threat jarred me. I stroked my belly and felt my world spinning. I nearly collapsed in front of her and begged her to leave me alone. If she wanted Kameel she could have him and be satisfied with him, but leave my child alone to me without taking any part of her.

I begged her silently, *"For God's sake, leave me alone!"*

CHAPTER 21

SABAH SETS THE STAGE ON FIRE

"**H**ONEY Bunny… Honey Bunny… Honey Bunny…"

Sabah the entertainer's laughter rang through the speakers before she appeared onstage with the opening to the song. Her right hand clasped one of the female contestants as she descended steps at the back of the stage swaying to the melody of the music; in her left hand was a young boy. The rest of the contestants came out behind her in pairs, male and female, and scattered around her in a random fashion. The girls' hair was styled like Sabah's, in pigtails. They were wearing pink dresses with butterflies on them, while the boys were dressed in olive shorts with white striped shirts topped with suspenders.

Sabah started singing: "*Where do I start, honey bunny, where do I start?/ With your strawberry lips, so pretty, so tart/ Give me a kiss, the light of my eyes/ They want to eat you up/ But they don't know where to start.*"

She mellifluously stretched out the words "Where do I start" as she flitted among the kids, who repeated the song after her. Around the kids stood dancers in huge bunny costumes, bopping to the beat of the music.

I searched for Omar on the TV screen as I ate popcorn, stretched out on the comfy living-room couch. He looked really cute as a young boy, just like I remembered him from my college days. He was the last to come onstage, holding the hand of a beautiful dark girl.

He seemed distracted to me as he followed the child who led him confidently towards the space designated for them. When they started singing, they all raised their voices as if they were competing in a yelling contest instead of singing. Omar wasn't comfortable in what he was wearing, annoyed at the child who was trying to grab him again and again whenever he let her hand go to scratch his behind. He lost his cool and on her last attempt shoved her away, causing her to fall. He continued singing as if nothing had happened. No one on the stage seemed to be aware of what he had done. The girl got up on her own and started singing again by his side without trying to grab his hand again. After the song ended, Hilda appeared on the right side of the stage and drew close to Sabah saying, "*They want to eat you up, honey bunny…* a new arrangement especially composed for our show. Welcome our dear artiste, pillar of humanity, the sweet Sabuha, here in Amman, the capital of Arab art and culture." Turning to Sabah, she asked, "What do you think of Amman?"

"Amman is amaaazing, and has been for all its life, like its beautiful people. I love Amman. A big hello to its people and the ruling family—I love them all! I greet King Abdallah and Crown Prince Hussein, and may King Hussein his grandfather rest in peace. I remember his reign very well, and Queen Noor, and also Queen Rania is one of the greatest. They're all awesome."

"It's been some time since you last visited Amman. Has it changed much?"

"Everything in Amman has changed. It's become even better! As soon as I arrived, I was surprised by the new towers, which made me realize I don't really know it at all."

Sabah laughed and added, "But the two towers they started on the sixth roundabout so long ago still haven't been finished. What a disappointment! They should make it into a museum or something... unlucky guys who made them."

"Well then, Sabuha, what do you think of our contestants?"

"They're so adorable! May God keep the evil eye away from them. God willing, they'll grow up again and live new lives in place of the hard days that they once endured. Every one of us has gone through tough days, but now we're in a simpler and sweeter age. Each of us is able to help people and pull them out of poverty while all our lives continue to improve."

"God willing, our lives will get better and better with you among us, your songs and your wonderful spirit," Hilda said. She turned to the audience and continued, "We've gotten closer to the end of our journey here on the show. Our contestants today have dialed back their ages to five years. In the next month, they'll have completed their journey of going back to the first day." Turning back to Sabah, Hilda said, "Sabuha's made a habit of being generous and kind. Today she has decided to adopt one of our participants, so she'll be with us during the final episode to choose the kid that she wants to adopt. Voting will be more competitive than ever, and the contestants will need *your* votes. You're the ones who'll decide who will be born again with a golden spoon. Decide, vote, and take part with us so we can give children new hope. Stay with us. We'll be back after the break."

A quick clip of the children singing came up on the screen, *Where do I start, honey bunny, where do I start?* before they were covered up by the show's logo, which then morphed into an image of a child winking at the crowd with a golden spoon in hand.

CHAPTER 22

CHUNKS OF FLESH

IT was tough for Zaid to transform from a man to an adolescent. His height shrunk, the size of his bones shrunk, his muscles lost mass, he lost facial and chest hair, and the pitch of his voice went up an octave. All of these changes left him terrified.

He would get up in the morning, get on the scale, and call out to me, "Janna, I've lost such-and-such kilos!" then straighten his back in front of the electronic wall and leave it to read his height. He would memorize the reading that it produced next to his image, and then make his way to the mirror. He'd take off his pajama top and scrutinize the size of his muscles, shoulders, and chest.

When I stood behind him, I was amazed at his body's rapid transformation. I found it difficult to comprehend my feelings for him when he was in this state, at this size, this age. I worried about him and would suggest, "Isn't this enough?" He never liked my suggestion and would immediately snap back, "No, it's not."

I knew how stubborn he was. I'd gotten used to him being

like that after making some decision or the other, and was familiar with his refusal to back down from his decision even if its consequences harmed him. But it wasn't easy for me at all. The changes that were happening to him weren't just physical. Morphological changes were accompanied by a mental shift that became apparent in his behavior, his reactions, and bases on which he began to make decisions.

Previously I had thought that accumulated life experiences and knowledge were what matured a person's personality, grew a respect for the latter stages of life, and lay the foundations of wisdom in old age. I doubted this idea when I started to see a number of those who had returned to their youth losing the maturity they had gained in years past. I myself tasted my own return to youth, though I still maintained some of the characteristics that had identified me as an elderly person.

As for Zaid, the changes that happened to him were so profound that sometimes I considered him to not have matured at all in his life. As if he hadn't lived on this earth longer than the thirteen years that his physical traits suggested, not ninety-five years that he had truly lived since the day he was born.

The certainty that the physical vessel of a human being was what carried our genetic code, personality, desires, and identity itself was what scared me.

In the past, the change in my mother's personality shocked me along with her growing loss of working brain neurons. This, as well as how Jamal's personality changed as he advanced in age. Now, the consequences of remodeling that physical vessel were apparent in Zaid's personality.

What scared me more than this was the truth that man now possesses a number of technologies that make it easier for him to control the biological shifts that tie his body to others of his kind and to those of the biological kingdom around him.

One of the strange technologies that was applied to repair marital relations involved linking the image of your life partner with hormone secretions in the brain. It's a simple technology that makes use of the e-lens that an individual wears. After identifying your life partner's face, it orders the nanobots that swim in our blood stream to make their way to the erotic locus of the brain and activate it.

A friend of mine tried it a few months before to reignite the spark in her dying marriage. She confessed to me that for a while she had been attracted to men who stood in absolute physical contrast to her husband. She was preparing to ask for a divorce when her marriage counselor suggested that she try the treatment out.

The last time we got together, she told me she had always loved her husband in some shape or form, but that the love she had felt before didn't compare to how much she loved him now. She said, "Janna, for a while now I had convinced myself that sex was a nonessential in a marriage that had gone on for years, and this always alarmed me. Today I'm no longer afraid, and my marriage is now complete after all these years."

Maybe this technology would work for me too. The idea put me at ease.

Embarrassed, I acknowledged that I was thinking of myself as I listened to her speaking so candidly about such a private matter. I didn't have the guts to share my story like she was doing, I had gotten used to denying the importance of sex in a marriage. I decided to keep my lips zipped and not tell her that she was repeating what I had gotten used to running away from, the voices that that rang out in my ears now and again.

I got lost in thought and imagined a reality where my feelings for Kameel didn't exist and were directed at Zaid instead. A vision of a reality where it was possible to put the spark back into our marriage, and rescue me from the divergent waves of feelings that pushed him away and pulled him close to me at the same time; an image of Zaid arousing me whenever I laid eyes on it, rendering me weak in the knees, leaving me crying from the intensity of the feelings that stormed within me – that kind of love.

Something within me was repulsed by this technology. There was something unnatural about it, about how it encouraged self-deception to change my feelings towards my husband. It might strengthen them, intensify them, but it wouldn't change my awareness that these feelings weren't and would never be real.

Maybe a part of me got used to the feelings as they were; it preferred things to remain as they were, natural, with their own special taste, even if they were less sharp than what I had tasted with Kameel.

The man-child state in which Zaid was stuck at the time wasn't really conducive to sexual attraction. It would have been useful for us to try that high-tech solution before his escape to childhood and before my obsession with giving birth to my mother intensified. Now, he was a child and I was in my third month of pregnancy. The talk of any kind of redemption of our sexual relationship was nothing more than a joke. Each of us had plunged deeply into a personal journey that altered our physical features and left us each fighting to get to know the new world we were experiencing. Two journeys on two separate trails in two different directions, with no meeting point for a conjugal relationship. We'd put it on the shelf until each of us came back to our natural state one day.

I didn't know which one of us was in a better state: he started getting up daily to record the changes that were happening to his body, whereas I would get up to eat berries.

The cravings that marked pregnancy had taken hold of me, birthing a strange love for berries that I hadn't experienced before. I used to ask for them all day, and late into the night as well. I'd carry a plate of berries with me and put it next to my bed before I slept. I'd stretch out my hand and pop one or two into my mouth whenever my eyes opened in the middle of the night. In the morning, I'd wake up to grab the plate and finish off whatever was left.

Despite the annoying morning sickness I had started to experience, the leftover berries were rarely enough. I'd push myself to get up quickly and make my way towards the food printer in the kitchen before I washed my face. I'd choose different types of berries and leave the printer to produce them. I'd prepare a cup of coffee while it finished. I'd sit opposite the printer and observe the berries taking shape before my eyes. I'd pick up what had already been printed and stuff them greedily, waiting impatiently for more to print.

My cravings weren't limited to a particular type of berry. During this period, I tasted all types; sometimes I preferred white, other times blue, and sometimes cranberries or black-berries or raspberries. New kinds appeared every day on the website that I bought them from. I'd order the raw materials from the store every week, and they'd arrive within the hour. I'd fill the printer with these materials and choose according to what I wanted: the type of berry, its color, how sweet or bitter, and the shape it should be printed in.

There were always crazy options and strange designs available, but I conservatively chose to just print them in their natural shape. I didn't like berries that tasted like bananas or coconuts, and I didn't like the weird-shaped berries that looked like figs, pomegranates, or oranges. I preferred them on the whole as they were, though I did order them extra bitter and larger than their usual size.

I didn't go to the office that day. I was feeling sluggish and preferred to stay at home. I was, as usual, compulsively printing berries in the kitchen when lunchtime rolled around. I prepared some food and waited for Zaid. He hadn't come out of the bedroom since the morning, after he'd gone back in after breakfast. I thought he was probably reading a book or watching some movie, or playing a videogame.

I called out to him, "Zaid!", but he didn't respond. I raised my voice further, "Zaid, food's ready!" No response. I yelled again after a few minutes, "Zaid, the food will get cold!", but he didn't answer.

I rushed to the bedroom and pushed open the door.

What I saw left me speechless.

While I had been printing berries in the kitchen, Zaid had been printing something else altogether. I saw the printer specialized in printing human body tissue and muscles that we had bought for Jamal being used for the first time.

Around me, everywhere on the floor were inflated balls of flesh in myriad shapes and sizes. Every two were stuck together and scattered everywhere. I didn't comprehend the scene in front of my eyes as I began to see perfect female breasts spread around my bedroom, on my clothes, on my bed, in between my perfume bottles, and around my make-up.

I couldn't understand the insanity that had struck Zaid. He was sitting quietly behind the desk stuck to the e-tablet covered with naked women and numerous options for breast designs on sale. The printer next to him on the desk was busily working on spitting out a new breast.

Trembling, I enquired, "Zaid, what *is* this?"

He didn't answer.

"Zaid, what on earth are you doing?" I repeated the question as I approached him.

"I'm printing."

"You're printing? What are you printing?" I asked him bitterly.

"What do you think?" he mocked me. He picked up a pair of breasts from the ground, put them in his lap, and began to fondle them.

I heard a twinge of sadness in his voice, and realized that he wasn't doing this to insult me, but he was reacting to the fear that had seized him. I reined myself in and changed the tone of my voice.

I went right up to him and placed my hands on his shoulders from behind. I let him turn his face away so that the meeting of our eyes wouldn't affect our feelings. We no longer had it in us to have a rational conversation. I asked him quietly, "Why are you printing breasts?"

He didn't answer. I sensed him trying to hold his tears back. I applied slight pressure with my fingertips on the nape of his neck and apologized: "I'm sorry for what happened this morning. I didn't mean it." He stayed silent, so I continued, "Didn't we agree to delay the whole sex thing until you grow back up again into an adult?"

"But I'm still your husband, I'm not a kid, I still feel, I can still…"

"I know that you can, it's just… I don't know…." I stopped talking, and I didn't know what to do. I felt his anger. I caressed his head and hugged him. I left him to calm down and kissed his forehead. I thought he was convinced by what I had said, and decided to leave it alone as we had decided earlier. But, just like he had done in the morning, stretched out his hands and started to fondle my breasts.

My reaction wasn't the nicest in the morning, but he shocked me with this move. This morning when he stretched out his hand in bed to hug me, I thought it was an innocent movement where he was trying to make me feel his love and his need for my tenderness. But he started to move his hands across my body in a clearly sexual manner. I didn't show any reaction at first, neither repelling him nor responding to his advances. I thought he would read my stiff body language and stop, but he kept on. The intensity of his hand movement grew and in a flash, I felt him turn his body and jump on top of me, occupied with kissing me.

He kissed me hungrily, and I still didn't respond. I moved my head to the right to distance my lips from his. I grabbed his arms and urged him to get away from me. His desire was too strong for him to understand that I was trying to resist him. He pressed up against me further trying to get even closer to me. This set me off and I couldn't control myself any further, and pushed him to the side violently.

I got up and left the room to him.

Now it was happening again.

Maybe he read my return, my kindness towards him, and my silence as a change of heart. I didn't want to reject him a second time after I felt that I had offended him right after seeing the breasts that he had printed. I let him keep on with his fondling. I tried to comply with him even though my body wasn't ready. His short height and small body size made me feel that I was with a child, not a man, and this repulsed me and killed my desire.

But I didn't reject him this time; I let him lead with no resistance from my end. He held my hand and pulled me to the bed, and there, among the piles of breasts, he did what he wanted.

CHAPTER 23

ZAID'S BUDDIES

I WAS like a swinging pendulum in the wind, rocking freely back and forth between Zaid and Kameel. I felt a weight distancing me from the meeting point with Zaid when Kameel was afar, and another weight in the opposite direction pulling me back to Zaid when I got close to Kameel and smelled his cologne. My collision with either of them would recharge me with a stabilizing energy that transmuted into force pushing me in the opposite direction.

I have always felt helpless before Mother Nature's laws. I used to think that only the laws of physics mattered, but now I realized that such laws also impacted emotions with the same logic and harshness.

Zaid's attempt to revive the sexual relationship between us while he was in this body angered me. He was provoking me in a manner that I hadn't confronted before, and it increased my desire to leave him and seek refuge with Kameel. My reaction to Zaid's provocations established a new way of interacting with him, one I hadn't experienced before. He had become a child in my view, and I started to feel the balance of power in our relationship shifting in my favor.

I started to look at myself as physically stronger and more socially and intellectually mature. I had to assume the leadership role and behave with the wisdom that corresponded with the amount of responsibility that had been thrown on my doorstep once Zaid decided to sail off on this adventure of his.

But he didn't make the task easy for me. It's like there was something within pushing him to assert his independence and masculinity whenever his height further dropped and his body shrunk. He had become an adolescent who lived recklessly, an adolescent who didn't know how to assert his existence without yelling and being short-tempered. And I'd become that mother who searched for ways to come to grips with the craziness of her child, to comprehend needs that she didn't understand.

He surprised me one day by bringing over a group of friends to the house without letting me know. I was watching TV in the living room, in my PJs, when he opened the door suddenly with a group of boys and girls in tow. They were all right about his size.

The glitter of the large golden crosses that adorned their chests caught my attention. Although I was not happy to have unannounced guests, I was also curious. I got a grip, stood up, and greeted them. I recognized Zaid's friend Isa among them, but I didn't know the rest. "How are you, Isa?" I inquired in a tone of voice that was a cross between the one I previously used to address him in as an adult, and the way I'd started talking to Zaid as of late.

"Praise be to God," he answered. He left Zaid to introduce me to the rest of the group.

Zaid pointed to the child behind Isa and said, "Isa's wife, Luma." Luma smiled as she took the lollipop out of her mouth and greeted me, "Hi." Zaid continued, "Isa's daughter Sara." Sara nodded. "Here is Isa's grandson, Fadi, and Huda, Fadi's sister," Zaid concluded.

There were lollipops in all their mouths. The girls had parted their hair down the middle and tied it in pigtails. As for the boys, they had left their hair tousled. All of them were wearing leather sandals.

They were a strange sight, as if they were striving to come across as younger than the physical age that their bodies had reached. It was as if they were acting out a juvenile quality that wasn't in them, in a desperate attempt to speed up their entry to the heavenly kingdom, as they believed.

I harbored some resentment towards the idea of returning to childhood after I found an echo of it in my house and started living with it through Zaid. But I also was intrigued to meet an entire family that had decided to sail in the sea of returning to childhood together. The father, mother, daughter, and grandchildren, all of them, on the same journey of adolescence that Zaid was on as well, and all of them living under the same roof!

I had planned for a while to visit the Christian-populated Fuheis and examine this phenomenon firsthand after news reports had begun to expose it, but I was yet to act on that plan. Churches had grown full of children, with child-priests leading them in daily mass, anticipating the end of the world. Sociological questions floated to the surface, trying to establish the capability of these societies of children and their sustainability, their ability to safeguard security and safety, and the economic cost that this phenomenon was now placing on the nation and on society as a whole.

Seeing them today in front of me made me wonder if Parliament would forbid childhood someday as well, just as it was trying to outlaw old age.

I put a few cushions on the ground in a circle so they could sit down. They were planning on playing cards, and Isa surprised me when he took out a pack of cards that reminded me of my childhood. Unexpectedly they held hands and recited after Isa a prayer from the Bible, "Our Father who art in heaven, hallowed be thy name, thy kingdom come, thy will be done, on earth as it is in heaven." Zaid and I left them to finish their prayer as we brought them some juice and popcorn from the kitchen.

Zaid sat among them and they started playing cards. I sat on the couch behind them, watching them with fascination. None of them had an e-lens on, and none of them was wearing a smartwatch, belt, or any other device. They had chosen to live simply, and it seemed to me that they were living happily.

Zaid also looked in high spirits among them. They were all absorbed in their game, laughing, shouting, exchanging cards and smiles, without any worries or responsibilities. They were chatting with each other without any deference to age, as if the grandson was a childhood friend of the grandfather and the granddaughter a childhood friend of her grandmother.

I lost myself in the surreal experience. I envied how happy they were. I was surprised at their ability to hope, their blind faith in the unknown, a full faith without doubt or further consideration. I remembered Jamal in that moment. I remembered his face at the time of his death. He was like them, with complete faith and limitless hope for a better life. I remembered Kameel as well, and missed him. I grew sad at my inability to have faith in something, and in my failure to hope.

CHAPTER 24

MOM, SHE'S MY HEAVEN

I DREW in brown a tree trunk on the right side of the paper. I drew its branches in green in the shape of puffy clouds. I put between the branches red circles that I wanted to be apples. I took a yellow marker and drew a sun to the right of the tree. I exaggerated the length of its rays.

Mom bent down beside me on small rug in the bedroom Jamal and I shared. She stretched out her hand, ruffled my hair, and asked, "What you drawing there, Junjun?"

My eyes glittered as I innocently answered, "A tree."

She took the paper from my hand, sat cross-legged on the ground, picked me up, and put me in her lap. She chose several markers and completed my picture: grass and flowers covering the bottom of the page; a blue sky with colorful birds drawn amateurishly at the top; on the side of the tree, a small wooden cabin surrounded by a blue river; and behind it, a rainbow reaching from the sun that I had drawn to the cabin she had drawn.

She offered me one of the markers and asked, "What's this picture missing?"

I knew what she meant. I took the marker from her hand and drew above the river a man and a woman, and to the side a boy on the right and a girl on the left.

Mom smiled. She pointed to the man and asked, "Who's that?"

"Dad."

She pointed to the woman: "Who's this?"

I giggled with childish shyness: "You."

She kissed my forehead and went on with her questions. She pointed to the boy and joked, "Is this Janna?"

I corrected her right away: "No, that's Jamal."

She laughed, pointed to the girl, and said enthusiastically, "Ahhhh, here's darling Janna, my sweetheart."

She put her hand under my armpit and started to tickle me. I burst out laughing as her fingers darted from spot to spot. I laughed until I lost my breath. I felt I couldn't laugh anymore, so she stopped a bit to let me catch my breath, and then started tickling me again. She pulled me to her chest after I had finished laughing. She brought the paper in front of me and asked, "Do you know what your name means?"

I didn't understand her question, and she didn't wait for my answer. She drew a circle with her finger to include everything that was on the paper. "You see all the great things in this picture? This here is heaven, and you, darling, are my heaven."

I wasn't sufficiently aware to respond to her at my five years of age, but I knew well enough that she, she was my heaven.

If only that moment could have come back to me, if only

I had raised my small hand, put it over her mouth, brought my lips close to her ear, and whispered, "I love you." But time doesn't come back, and its sweet moments, even if they resemble one another when repeated, all that is left of them is their individual impressions and tastes.

My hand doesn't extend to my mother's mouth today, but it reaches to my stomach instead, where it is now capable of transferring my love to her with a tender touch, in response to her kicks. My lips also may not be able to see her ears to whisper into them, but they're able to hum melodies that express my love for her in another way as she rocks to them.

I may one day, when Amal gets close in age to my mother's age at that one moment in time, repeat Zaid's craziness and go back to my childhood. I would then drink in the vision of my mother and sit in her lap. I'll put my hand on her mouth a second time, sidle up to her ear, and whisper once more, "I love, you, I love you, I love you, I love you."

Time has changed, unsettling the heaven that we had drawn together, but that moment with her was imprinted in my mind; it was still alive just like that drawing she had saved, now in my wardrobe drawer.

Among one of her most surprising characteristics was her ability to keep things that mattered to her. Whether it was a shoe, a dress, or a cooking utensil, my mother was devoted to what she owned. Things took on a special meaning in her presence. She would love them, grasp them, and not exchange them unless she was sure she couldn't use them in some other way. Her favorite saying in life, "A bird in the hand is worth more than ten in the bush," she repeated to me whenever the bird that was in my hand lost its sparkle and ten in the bush faraway called out to me. She would repeat it to me, trying to instill in me the value of contentment. She'd add to the previous saying and recite, "Contentment is an everlasting treasure."

But contentment wasn't to find an everlasting place in my heart. It would visit me for a few simple moments before it dissipated. It would leave me tormented, longing for what was far from me, as if things that were far from me had a distinct sheen, losing that gleam and becoming dull and meaningless when I touched them and brought them close to me. I learned from Mom to hold onto things and not waste them, but I didn't inherit her contentment.

With time, I learned to adapt my concept of contentment to joy in what I had, to joy in what I didn't have. Those things that shimmered around me, lighting up my world, were far from me. My longing for them nagged at me, but it would supply me with the motive to work and reach them. I knew that their shine would disappear the moment I got hold of them, making my arduous journey meaningless, but I knew also that this type of deception was necessary to provide me with a motive to live, and the ability to wake up every day to work at getting nearer to that dream.

Life without dreams is meaningless, and the beauty of a dream is that it's only an illusion and not real. When life becomes as drawn out as it is today, and wishes become easy to achieve, then dreams become strange, crazy, worthless, and illogical, just like the stars in the sky, their beauty lying in their remoteness and the impossibility of reaching them.

Chapter 25

Forbidden Fruit

I TOSSED violently from side to side in bed the night after Kameel kissed me. As if a radiant light had illuminated my consciousness, my thoughts were paralyzed, and I fell prisoner to strange feelings. I had let Zaid fall asleep in my arms after I had reassured him of my love and commitment. But my body wouldn't sleep. It was burning up, demanding Kameel.

His kiss tormented me while my conscience gnawed at me. I wasn't used to betraying Zaid, and I wasn't going to let myself betray him after all these years of marriage. Abandoning him in this adolescent state wasn't something I could do. I couldn't leave him when he was in the peak of manhood, and I wouldn't be able to do it when his manhood eventually came back to him. I knew that he was predestined for me by fate, so I wouldn't betray him and I wouldn't leave him.

But my body was demanding what was forbidden. Fortunately, time had taught me how to deal with such urges. It had become customary that whenever desire overcame me and I couldn't find my husband around to sort it out, I would rush to the bathroom, lock the door behind me, and give my body what it needed. Just like dreams and the stars in the sky, I had a copy of Kameel in my imagination. One that I could reach and not reach, that I could have and not have, that I could hold without touching him. I enjoyed Kameel from the required distance, not satisfying myself with him, and his image didn't lose its shine.

I filled the bathtub with hot water and took off my nightshirt and my underwear. I lay down inside, panting with desire. Kameel's image as he kissed me played on my mind, but I wanted to see his face in greater clarity. I blinked my eyes to rotate the projector to the wall. I searched among publicly available photos of Kameel and projected a picture in which he was looking especially hot on the wall, and then enlarged it so it would be as if he was right in front of me.

I got lost in my thoughts, replaying the scene of the kiss and embellishing it. I moved projected-Kameel around as I wished and was aroused by his movement. I thought of him as taller, and raised my gaze upwards. My being older than him increased my attraction to him. His youth lent him a quality of purity, or maybe superiority, in my subconscious. His interest in me, and his attraction to me, made me feel increasingly feminine, or maybe it was the lack of rationality of this relationship and my refusal to give in physically to someone all those years younger than me that increased his appeal and exaggerated my arousal.

He carried me like a child in his arms to bed, and spread his body out over mine. He controlled me with his presence, and I was unable to breathe.

This was all in my imagination. As for me, I moved my hand under the water to reach my G-spot and gasped. I opened my eyes to steal a clearer look at Kameel on the wall in front of me. I closed them again and applied even greater pressure as I imagined what could be. I felt Kameel enter me, and felt my excitement increase. I kept on imagining until bursts of bliss dazzled me like lightning from the sky. They left me quiet, wandering, catching my breath, far from Kameel and his arousal of my body.

I cleaned up and wiped myself down. I returned to the bedroom and got into bed again beside Zaid. He was fast asleep, but I felt the desire to hug him. I put one hand under his head and brought it close to mine. I hugged him with my other hand. I kissed his forehand and murmured, "Don't worry." I held his hand, squeezed it, and slept.

CHAPTER 26

THE FINAL EPISODE

CHILDREN'S strollers were lined up next to each other on stage. Each stroller carried a baby. Each baby boy was wrapped up in a blue blanket and each baby girl in a pink one. Behind each stroller was a man or woman in nurse's clothes, representing each child. The strollers had come in from different corners of the stage to the sound of lullabies. The host didn't introduce the babies until they had all arrived and the show's logo appeared on the screen.

Hilda walked a few steps to stand in the middle of the strollers. Directing her speech to the audience, she said, "It is truly a one-of-a-kind experience that our contestants have had during the last few months. You, our viewers, have got to know them up close, and you've watched the pain each has gone through in their previous life. You've connected with them, loved them, and followed their gripping journey on their way back to childhood.

"Today, our participants have gone back to their first day of life… and tonight, each of them will have a new shot at life. There's hope. There's joy. The team here on the show came together to offer support to ensure all the contestants get full healthcare and school fees paid for until they reach adulthood. But today one of them, based on your choice tonight, will win fifty million dinars. Your choice tonight will determine which contestant will be born again, with a golden spoon in his mouth."

I was sitting in the audience, in the front row, following the episode, fatigued from the swelling of my stomach from the fourth month of pregnancy. Zaid was sitting on my left, small in stature after finishing his own adventure back to the age of ten. On my right was Sabah, also following the show.

Even though we were in the first row from the stage, our view of the children was limited. I was dying to have a close-up look of Omar, hoping that he would be the lucky millionaire. I focused my gaze on him so that the e-lens would activate and zoom in on his image, but the angle of my vision from my seat wasn't great. A close-up shot of his face appeared fleetingly on the screens spread throughout the set. My heartbeat sped up when I saw his angelic face and his tiny fingers balled into a fist. I almost yelled, *What have you done to yourself, Omar?* I was disheartened.

Hilda welcomed Sabah, a number of other celebrities present on set, and me, before she moved on to the next segment of the show.

"Viewers, I'll leave you with this brief report of the contestants' journey on this show, and afterwards there's a short break. When we return we'll read the contestants' wills for their future lives and we'll see which child Sabuha has chosen to adopt."

I almost asked Sabah if she had chosen Omar, but I stopped short, shy. She took me by surprise with her question, "It's a girl, right? Praise be to God, how wonderful you look! Pregnancy really suits you."

I laughed and thanked her for her sweet words, which hit the nail on the head.

"How far along are you?"

"Four months."

"Fabulous, may God strengthen you, darling, and ensure you give birth safely. Have you heard how people are saying they're going to have kids now?"

I didn't catch her drift. I shook my head.

She went on incredulously, "Oh honey, haven't you heard? Instead of getting pregnant and having kids, the new 'in thing' is to print kids."

"Ahhh… people have really lost it!" I chimed in with her disapproval of the whole thing.

She laughed and added, "For a while, they've been saying that I'm crazy, but these days there's no sane person left."

She turned her face to the stage as if recollecting faded memories. She looked at me and giggled, "Argh, if only I could've printed ten of my former husband Rushdy Abaza, oh goodness!"

Hilda cut us off at the end of the commercial and called Sabah to the stage. "Sabuha, our viewers are waiting with bated breath! They'd like to know who you've chosen to adopt?"

Sabah's gaze roamed between the strollers. It hovered on the side where Omar's stroller was, and she started to walk towards him determinedly. My heart raced as she approached him, and I hoped that he would be the lucky one. But she passed him and approached the baby girl in the stroller next to him instead. Sabah picked her up gently and returned to finish talking with Hilda to the sound of warm applause.

"Salma! Sabuha's chosen Salma! Salma, dear viewers, is the lucky one Sabuha has adopted!" Hilda exclaimed as the theatre screens lit up with photos of Salma at different ages.

After the audience had quieted down a bit, Hilda asked Sabah, "Why Salma?"

"I don't know… she made her way into my heart. I've loved her from the very first episode. This poor girl had a rough life… I pray God gives me strength to make it up to her and give her a better one."

"Sabuha, we know that, prior to Salma growing young, there was an agreement between Salma and yourself that you'd adopt her. You also agreed on something else as well. Would you like to share with the audience what that is?"

"Salma wanted to start afresh. She even wanted her name to be something else," Sabah responded, her voice tinged with sadness.

"Okay, so what's the new name that you and Salma decided on?"

Sabah was quiet for a moment, as if she was hesitant to answer, before she surprised the audience by saying "Huwaida."

"After your own daughter, may she rest in peace."

"Thank you."

Sabah then went on hesitantly, "Maybe you know, Hilda, and the audience as well, that I shortchanged my daughter

Huwaida. I was distracted by my music and fame at the time I had her. As much as I tried to give her my time, and make up for my busyness, I wasn't able to guarantee her the emotional safety she needed. This time will be different. I'll take a break from my career, an extended holiday until she's grown and no longer needs me... maybe God's giving me a second chance just like He's given her. God willing, I'll be able to give her the happiness that I couldn't give Huwaida."

"We're confident that you'll make her happy like you've made us through your songs and sweet spirit all these years." Hilda then turned to the crowd. "Sabuha announces a long hiatus from performing onstage. You heard it here first, on *Born Again with a Golden Spoon*. A big salute to Sabuha for her great humanity, generosity, and values... a quick ad break and we'll be back to continue the show."

Sabah's words on stage moved me. I stood, along with the whole audience, in ovation. I waited for her to descend from the stage and make her way back to her seat next to me. My body was trembling, overcome with emotion when I hugged her to congratulate her. I almost told her that, like her, I too had struggled with nostalgia for the days gone past. I was trying to bring back my mother just like she was trying to bring back her daughter.

I got lost in trying to comprehend the power of the bond between mother and child, which circumstances can't change and time can't erase. Hilda's voice pulled me out of my contemplation, calling my name.

"Janna Abdallah, the writer, can you please make your way to the stage."

Her invitation took me by surprise but I stood confidently and made my way to the right-hand side of the stage. I went up the few steps, approaching her while the audience clapped.

"Welcome Janna a second time to our show. As you know, Omar left a will for his future life before he entered the stage of childhood. The document that contains his will is in your hand right now. We'd like you to please read it aloud."

I opened the paper slowly, curious to read Omar's will. I brought the mike that Hilda had given me closer to my mouth, and started to read aloud: "Mama Janna, I'm sure this is a shock for you. The team here at the show asked us to write a will that outlines our future lives or any wishes that we want to come true. When you read this letter I'll be in a diaper, not knowing anything anymore, not even my name. Today I'm confident that if I searched for someone to be my mother in this new life to come, I wouldn't come across anyone better or tenderer than you. I know you don't have kids. For so long I prayed that God would bless you with a child to bring you joy. Today my prayer has come true in a roundabout way; maybe I'm the child that I had prayed for you for. I know what I'm asking of you isn't easy, but I hope you'll agree… and be my mother."

Chapter 27

A Mother's Choice

I **CHANGED** Omar's diaper and dressed him in a white shirt and striped cotton pants. I held his feet, kissed them, enjoying his reaction. He was laughing with a joy that made my heart pulse, the innocent laughter of a three-month-old child getting to know the world afresh. I held his feet again, kissing them a second, third, and fourth time before I put them in socks and concerned myself with breast-feeding him.

Zaid stood beside me, playing with Omar. I asked him for the third time to go to his room and get dressed while I finished feeding Omar so that we wouldn't be late for the gathering in front of Parliament to oppose the law banning suicide.

As if I hadn't asked him at all, he kept playing with Omar. A minute later, he told me in a sugary voice, "I want a Nutella sandwich."

"Didn't you just eat one? Come on, go get dressed and finish up. I'll feed Omar and then I'll make your sandwich."

The tension of being in my seventh month of pregnancy had taken complete hold over me: my back ached, the weight of my stomach exhausted me, my breathing had become heavier and my sides were swollen. Just taking care of Omar alone took a huge amount of effort, and that's why I couldn't stand to entertain Zaid. I tried to control my nerves, but I lost it sometimes, especially when his troublesome behavior coincided with Omar's crying.

I had hit Zaid for the first time the day before, and I felt my conscience tugging at me. I had asked him several times to remove the bunch of cars that he played with from the hallway so that I wouldn't stumble over them on my way to the bedroom, but he failed to do so. I also asked him to keep the cars away from Omar's play area so that he wouldn't chew on them, but Zaid did just the opposite. Even before that, I'd asked him to shower and put on his PJs after he came home dirty, stinking of sweat from playing soccer in the neighborhood, but he ignored me.

I lost it when I saw Omar holding that toy car and sucking on it. I shuddered with alarm. I rushed and forced my finger into his mouth to search for the car. I pulled it out, seething with anger at Zaid. I left Omar bawling, grabbed my sandal, and whacked Zaid on the butt. Then I pulled him to our room and shut the door on him.

I returned to Omar, cradled him, and cried along with him. When Omar had calmed down, I went to Zaid's room and apologized to him. On this day, I was trying to atone for what I had done by giving him everything he asked for.

When Hilda surprised me onstage with Omar's will, I didn't know how to respond. I hadn't comprehended the difficulty of the responsibility that was being thrown on my doorstep. I stood baffled for some moments, unable to imagine the meaning of such a request. The audience's silence increased the terror of the moment. It was as if time had stopped in front of me and everything around me had frozen up. I felt slightly dizzy and nearly fell down onstage. Hilda's voice brought me to my senses as she asked, "It's up to you, Janna. Tell us, do you agree to Omar's request or not?"

I kept things short by smiling widely to avoid embarrassment on stage and answered, "Of course it would be an honor to be your mother, Omar." I looked at Hilda and added, "You know, Hilda, I've never had a child in my life, and now I'm four months pregnant... yes, all of it is unexpected, but I'm sure Amal in my womb will be happy to have an older brother looking out for her. I lost my brother Jamal three months ago, and I know very well what it means for a girl to have a brother."

As soon as I had finished speaking, the stage crew pulled Omar's stroller out of line and brought it to me. I looked at him up close and my heart went out to him. A momentary feeling of motherhood towards him overcame me. I reached down and pulled him out of his stroller, carried him in my arms, and hugged him to my chest under the glaring stage lights and to the sound of the crowd applauding and whistling.

I felt an unprecedented transformation happen to my body when I held him again that night in my arms in the living room. It was as if Mother Nature herself had felt what had happened and prepared me for this moment. My breasts swelled up in a way I had never experienced before. I looked at my shirt and saw a few drops of liquid had soaked through. Even though I was still in my first few months of pregnancy and I didn't think that my breasts would be ready to lactate, I felt milk oozing out of my nipples. Later, I read that it was called colostrum – thick milk that resembles cream that comes before the breasts start to produce mother's milk.

But then, milk was streaming out of my breasts, and Omar's mouth searching for food was a few centimeters away from them. I didn't think about the weirdness of the situation at the time or Omar being a stranger to me. I let myself be carried away by the call of Mother Nature. I brought him close to me and was joyful at the eagerness with which he searched for nourishment. I breastfed him as if it was one of the most normal things I had ever done.

A strange feeling came over me now whenever I looked at him. I had a duty towards him that I never felt towards anyone else before. Even if he didn't win the grand prize on the show, he won me, so I had to prove to him that I was worth more than those millions.

Sometimes it seemed to me that his past was nothing more than an illusion, a dream or figment of the imagination, and that this illusion was only found in my head to motivate me so that I would work tirelessly to take care of him and ensure his comfort and happiness. I had created a new reality for myself. Omar was my son, he didn't have a previous life, and he hadn't suffered before. This would be the only life that he would ever know. And me? I would make sure that he would only see love, joy, and more joy.

I breastfed him and propped him over my shoulder, walking with him so that he would burp. I made a Nutella sand-wich for Zaid with Omar on my shoulder, and then I called out to Zaid. He came quickly, already dressed and ready to leave. I asked him to put his hat on so he wouldn't get sun-burnt. I dressed Omar in a crocheted white top. I put him in his stroller. I made sure to bring everything we'd need in the few hours outside: Omar's food, his diapers, and a change of clothes. I opened the door and left Zaid to drag the stroller out as he wanted, and the four of us were off together.

The street was teeming with people when we reached Parliament in al-Abdali. It was a sunny day on a spring after-noon in May, laced with a refreshing breeze. The crowd was split in two. One group was supporting the decision, standing on the curb next to the assembly; those opposed stood on the opposite curb of the street. I searched for a patch that was still uncrowded among those opposing. I found a free olive tree. I pulled Omar's stroller towards it and warned Zaid, "Stay around here. Don't go too far."

On the side of the street next to those opposing was a collection of symbolic coffins. Lying inside each of them was a man or woman acting as a corpse. On the end of each coffin was a makeshift headstone with the names of real people on them, with their actual birth and death dates:

Huda Mohammed Abd-Rahman (1980-2053)

73 years

Mohammed Abd-Karim (1965-2027)

62 years

Wala Adil Mustafa (1930-1985)

55 years

Atop the coffins fluttered a large banner; on it was written in wide letters:

The natural age for a human rarely goes over 100 years.

Death is our right, death is our choice, death is our freedom.

A group of the protestors wore shirts emblazoned with different messages: "Death is sacred," "I'm free," "I want to grow old," "Youth is a passing phase, don't get stuck," "Old age is dignified," etc. They were yelling in one voice, "Death is a choice and life is a choice… and we have the right to choose!" I raised my voice to yell with them as I read to myself the banners of the group across from us: "Old age is a sickness that depletes our country's resources," "Death is God's fate, not a choice," "You didn't have the right to choose life when you came into this world. Why do you think you've got the right to choose death?"

They were yelling, "*Haram, haram, haram*, suicide is forbidden!" I noticed Kameel standing beside Jihan on the curb facing us. His height set him apart from the rest of the group, amplifying his attractiveness. The both of them were wearing sunglasses that partly blocked their line of vision; I was also wearing my own pair, so I avoided raising my hand to greet them over the distance between us. But Kameel spotted me a few moments later and raised his hand to greet me. For a moment I wasn't sure if he was waving at me or at someone behind me. I raised my hand haltingly to respond to him. Jihan was standing at his side looking in my direction without any reaction as if she hadn't seen me at all, or was ignoring me. She pulled at him after a few moments and they both disappeared into the crowd.

Minutes later, a large group of protestors arrived clad in black T-shirts with skeletons printed on them. Each of them was holding a cane topped by a human skull. This new group thrust around wildly, which heightened Zaid's curiosity to find out what was in one of the coffins they carried. He drew closer to inspect it firsthand. They were like a suicide group trampling over one another, carelessly colliding into whoever was around them. I found myself yelling in irritation when one of them crashed into Zaid, pushing him over as he went on his way: "You wackos, there are kids here!"

I asked the young man standing next to me to keep an eye on Omar as I rushed to make sure that Zaid wasn't hurt. I helped him get up and asked if everything was okay. I checked his body once over to ensure he was free from any broken bones or deep wounds. His right hand was raw from a light graze on it. I held him and we returned to our spot under the tree. I rummaged around in my bag for a tissue, moistened it with some antiseptic, and disinfected Zaid's wound. I told him not to leave my side.

I sat on a wooden chair beside the tree, taut with tension.

It worried me, having my children in a place where coffins were being carried, a place swarming with manic, obsessive young people holding human skulls. I had come here today to honor Jamal, not out of love for old age. My presence was to defend freedom, not a death wish.

I looked at the large image of Jamal that I had raised above Omar's stroller and I remembered the tragedy of the night he passed. How difficult it had been for me to lose him that day, and how painful those weeks after his departure had been. Omar's laugh reverberated in my ear as he interacted with a young man who was standing next to his stroller and playing with him. I heard Zaid's sigh as he sat cradling his injured arm. Amal's light kicking in my womb brought me back to reality.

It was as if all of a sudden I had realized my real desire, one which I was trying to deny out of respect for Jamal's insistence on defending the freedom of choice. Even though I had always seen an individual's life as a personal right, that only he had the freedom to do what he wanted with it, I found myself that day motivated by a mother's selfishness. A mother who didn't see justice in the death of her children, even if it that death manifested itself in the curtailing of their freedom to choose. I'd become a mother ready to take on the world to gain even one extra moment to spend with Zaid, Omar, or Amal. I'd become a mother who didn't see anything wrong with stripping my children of their right to choose between life and death.

In that moment, I swore to myself that I wouldn't stand helplessly by any of their deathbeds; I wouldn't repeat that night when Jamal died.

I threw my shoulders back and stood up straight despite the weight of my stomach. I raised my head with confidence in my decision to choose life. I looked over at Zaid and said, "Follow me."

I held onto Omar's stroller and crossed the road to the other side. I stood there dignified, content with my ability to overcome my principles for the sake of what I really wanted. After a few minutes I found myself yelling, "*Haram, haram, haram*, suicide is forbidden!"

CHAPTER 28

HEAVEN ON EARTH

A S soon as the demonstration began to peter out,
Kameel popped up from among the crowd. He approached me and shook my hand. He shook Zaid's
hand as well and greeted him. He asked me what had been
behind my move to the opposite side of the road to this side,
in support of the law. He then complimented me on my dar-
ing to make such a decision, and my courage to cover the
distance between the two groups, each passionately defending
their own stance. He informed me that the votes were in, and
it had been decided in the corridors of Parliament in our favor. He invited me to celebrate with a group of the victors in
the Jabal al-Qal'a café, the citadel café perched atop one of
Amman's many hills.

It was tough for me to turn down Kameel's request, especially when he had asked so kindly. It was even more difficult
for me in that moment to not respond to my escalating feelings of attraction to him, his victory making him even more
handsome. But I was tired, and I didn't know if it was the
right thing to go with them with the kids in tow or not.

But he insisted. He turned to Zaid, trying to get him on his side: "Zaid, what do you think? Have you tried their ice cream? It's delicious!" He held Omar's stroller and began to pull it. "Let's go, Janna, don't drag your feet. After all, I'm sure Amal also wants some ice cream."

I gave in and walked behind him tentatively until I caught sight of Jihan standing in the group getting ready to go to the café. She saw me as well and started towards us. She approached us, head held high but without looking at me. She looked at Zaid when the distance had closed between us, and gasped, "Zaid? What have you done to yourself? I didn't recognize you!" She shook his hand and hugged him. She left him and closed in on Omar's stroller. She stood silently looking at him, and then bitterly commented as she laughed, "Three, Janna? *Three?* God help you!"

She turned her full attention to me and asked, "How's the pregnancy? How far along are you?"

"Seven months."

"God be praised, stay strong. The whole family is excited to see the baby."

I wasn't at ease talking to her, especially not with her questions about my baby girl, Amal. She was talking to me with a commanding tone as if she were in charge of me and my child!

"Are you all coming along with us?" she asked, not even waiting for an answer. She turned to Zaid, gestured towards the meeting point by the bus, and said, "Come on, Zaid, everyone's meeting up there. Follow me and don't take too long!"

It took us fifteen minutes to get to the Amman citadel.

Jihan chose a table looking out over the city, and we all sat down around it as if we were one big family, as if there wasn't a court case pending at that very moment. Jihan didn't speak to me much, and I also tried to avoid speaking to her. I left her to interrogate Zaid about his journey back to childhood and the feelings that he had been experiencing during that journey.

Omar was fast asleep when Kameel left to go the washroom by the café entrance.

The sky was clear that day, and the weather beautiful. The sun was setting as usual towards the west. The city seemed silent from our location at the top of the hill. Nothing pierced its tranquility except for the surrealist painting that the birds in the sky had drawn. The city's history was reflected in its buildings, the old and new, lumped together randomly to form the unique Amman landscape. Downtown were towering skyscrapers and on the hills the low-rise buildings that captured Amman's past.

In the past, I would feel small; I would bow to the eternity of the daily sun setting in front of me now. I used to consider myself a transient visitor, a faded whisper in the course of time, a beam of light that would fade in no time. But in that instance, I found myself present and celebrating my long-lived existence, just like this city, and just like the sky.

Jihan's voice broke into my daydreaming as she played with Omar. I looked at her and muttered to myself, "Jihan, just like always, pulling me back to reality."

It might be my destiny to be locked up with her here in this time, and days might go by while she prepared to get back at me. She might pull me apart from the ones I loved, and might steal from me those dearest to me. But I'd prepare a comeback for her too, I'd be her match, and I'd always remind myself, *If she's Hell-lady then I'm heaven, and if she's chosen to live on this earth, then I'll be heaven on this earth.*

As soon as I had decided to be the heaven that I had hoped to be, a terrifying sound – a great explosion – rocked me as it shook the city below.

People around me rushed to the edge of the hill, each trying to figure out the source of the explosion. A few moments later, that first explosion was followed by a second, third, and fourth. The flames of the ensuing fire stretched across the city sky like a scene from some sci-fi movie. Fear struck everyone and their screams rose as they tried to get in touch with their relatives at the suspected bomb sites to ensure they were okay.

As for me, I jumped up and huddled with Zaid and Jihan. Jihan was petrified, clutching Omar to her chest. I held her hand and hugged Zaid.

The sound of another explosion reverberated closer this time, and I felt my body fly up in the air and fall a meter behind. My back hurt when I hit the floor, but I suppressed my cry of pain and let out instead a roar, "Omar! Zaid!"

Zaid was splayed out a few steps away from me. He wasn't injured, and standing up, he came towards me. As for Omar, he was still protected in Jihan's embrace. She hadn't let him fall despite her being knocked back and falling to the ground, herself.

I sighed and felt somewhat calm, reassuring myself of their safety, but then I remembered Kameel and yelled, "Jihan! Kameel?" At her silence, I started crying, wailing, "No

Kameel… no…"

I tried to get up but couldn't. The pain in my back intensified and seemed to travel to my stomach. I yelled for help, and Jihan came to me. She grabbed my hand and asked which part of me hurt. Due to the severity of the pain, I couldn't speak, and said with great difficulty, "Jihan… I'm in labor."

Moments later, I felt the gushing of liquid between my legs. I screamed out of fear, trying to catch my breath in between the pains of delivery. Jihan called out for a doctor from those present. No one came forward.

I had almost passed out from the pain when Kameel appeared, his face smeared with blood. He rushed to me to check I was okay. He told everyone to step back so that I could breathe. He grabbed me by the shoulders and told me that I was in safe hands. He said he had trained for delivery during a nursing course he took during his time in college.

"Janna, don't worry. I'm here. We'll deliver Amal together." He immediately asked for a pot of hot water and put a pillow under my back. He held my hand and started to breathe with me, "One, two, three, ooof! One, two, three, ooof!" until I felt Amal find her way into this world.

I felt her come out of my womb and see the light. I heard her howling in Kameel's hands, and I relaxed. She was in safe hands. I let myself drift off.

CHAPTER 29

THE END

TWENTY years passed. The terrorist strike left our sense of security shattered, and it was a tough period for the country. It reminded us of the imminence of death and made us aware of humanity's ability to build and destroy. It brought back to us a scene from the near past where terrorist groups fomented chaos across the Arab world. We'd entered into a new round of conflict with fighting terrorism and it left us prisoners to the chaos of this world.

Man is strange: despite his feats of scientific and societal progress, his search for the best the earth has to offer, his construction of skyscrapers, his control over the diseases that used to wipe us out, and his escape from the short life that used to define his existence on earth, here he is, still prisoner to ideologies able to move him from heaven to hell in the blink of an eye.

I, too, was a prisoner to this epoch. I became aware of how I was now a mother to three children whom the world had thrown in my lap with its customary nonchalance, leaving me to protect them.

The violent nature of the events brought me closer to Jihan, who had obtained a ruling in her favor. All my worst fears came true the day she knocked on my door, a decision from the court ordering shared custody of Amal in her hand. She was convinced that I would have to share my child with her just as it had happened with Jamal, and as the days went by I began to see a glimpse of her in Amal. Even though Amal's genetic makeup was taken from my mom, she grew up as an individual, a spitting image of my mom, with a little of my soul and a lot of the spiciness that made Jihan who she was. Jihan taught Amal to call her Mama and carved out a unique relationship with her that I still feel jealous of today.

Amal saw something in Jihan that I was unable to see. She defended her whenever I treated Jihan like a fool, and insisted that Jihan had a kind heart hidden behind her tyrannical ways. It was as if she had drunk the same potion that Jamal tasted the day that he set sights on Jihan for the first time. Amal loved her, respected her, and admired her. Maybe she gleaned personality traits from Jihan that I was lacking, like her straightforwardness, her boldness, how she did not back down if she needed or wanted something; or maybe it was my increasing apprehension and continual worry that pushed her to search for a replacement, one that would put greater confidence in her identity and in her being. Having said all this, even though I wanted to run away from these traits of Jihan's, I got used to them and loved them in Amal.

As for Omar, he was the apple of my eye and king of my heart. Every day, I would make it up to him for his past life. I showered him with what he needed and what he didn't. I'd made a mini-bougie out of him, lists of designer brands rolling off his tongue more easily than country names. I used to smile whenever I saw him grumble about being bored or getting irritable due to his lack of patience, or trying to get out of something he was tasked with doing.

He simultaneously resembled his old self and not at all: lighthearted and filled with joie de vivre, but with an air of aristocracy far from the ascetic mien he'd once exuded. I never for one day tried to get him to recognize his past, but rather I left him to grow into a new mold with a new love for life. I find him today taller than he used to be, a sparkle in his eyes that wasn't there before.

As for my relationship with Zaid, it was even more complicated. It was difficult for us to comprehend the enormous shift in our relationship from one of marriage to one of a parent and child. We got into a lot of fights and we needed long-term counseling to get our relationship back to what it used to be. We made use of the biotechnological therapies to encode feelings in our psyche that strengthened our marital relationship, and despite that we still continued to be, as we always were, going through alternating bouts of emotions that brought us together and which drew us further apart from time to time. And to this day, I ask myself if he's the right person for me or not!

Kameel left a few weeks after I gave birth to Amal. After she had gotten bored with him, Jihan left him. I think that he migrated to Australia, and we have lost touch since. Neither one of us tried to contact the other, as if a light beam had passed through my life twice, once in the form of his grandfather and once as he is now, and then disappeared.

Now look, I'm still here, in this world, trying to understand the weird things that the world throws in our path every day. My yearnings for the past sometimes take over and sometimes a hope for a happier future envelops me. But I'm here, and I'll be here, like I was and will be, as heaven, Janna, on earth.